A Coffin
for
Callahan

Haydon Rochester, Jr.

Copyright © 2016, 2021

ISBN 9781523922680

Author's Note

A Coffin for Callahan is a work of fiction. While I hope the characters herein seem true to life, they are not based on real persons, living or dead, and any such impression is pure coincidence. The historic murder stories in this book are based on real events from the past of the Eastern Shore of Virginia, but the names have been changed in the interest of creating a fictional world. Likewise, the names of some localities have been changed to support the fictional nature of the story.

I would like to express my gratitude for the significant assistance provided by Miles Barnes and the staff of Eastern Shore Public Library. Other sources of assistance and inspiration include Janet Rochester, Roland Stahl, Peter Dundon, and Wikipedia. While this work would never have come into being without the contributions of these people and organizations, I accept all blame for any shortcomings.

Cover design and illustration by the author.

Onancock, Virginia
December 1, 2021

Also by Haydon Rochester, Jr.

Runabout

A Life in a Day

A Shirt Story & Other Short Stories

Night Bus to Progreso

The Old Switcheroo & Other Stories

Death Assemblage

The Boy Who Tricked the Wind

The Fire This Time

Walker's Guide for the Virginia Eastern Shore

First

Ed Callahan hated Tuesdays. It was on a Tuesday, roughly six months ago, that his wife Doris died in indescribable pain from breast cancer. In truth, since her death, Callahan hadn't been particularly fond of any day of the week. He'd tried to accept her passing, but his attempts at adjustment had yielded only a moderately efficient bachelor life. He handled the preparation of nutritious meals for one, doing the washing and ironing, and keeping the house fairly neat. His neighbor across the street, the widow Mrs. Davis, told him almost daily that he would make an ideal husband. He kept his house cleaner than most single women, she said. "Cleanliness is next to godliness," she also said—many times.

Most days of the week but Sunday, Callahan visited the Main Street Bakery, an easy walk from his home in Port St. George, Virginia. He enjoyed his visits to the morning coffee group there, where he would slowly consume a large chocolate chip cookie, carefully cutting it with a plastic fork into bite-size pieces, which he washed down with black coffee from a God Bless America paper cup. While there, he enjoyed his chats with the regulars about the latest town news, local and state politics, sports happenings, and the troubles of the world. He also looked forward to seeing some of the irregulars, such as the young historian Delbert Mason Dix, who stopped in two or three days a week. In cooler or rainy weather, Callahan often went from the bakery to the Fair Deals Hardware store, where he could usually count on joining a game of Hearts by the wood

1

stove to keep busy until it was time to go home for lunch. His evenings were spent watching television, except the occasional Friday night, when he would stop to play pool at the firehouse. As a retired cop, he was welcomed by the firemen and other first responders who hung out there. His life was a pleasant one, and it had been about as perfect as it could be—until Doris died.

Callahan realized he should be beginning to get over her death by now. At sixty, he had lived long enough to see many friends and relatives die. Doris had lived to fifty-nine, young for passing these days, but certainly well within the portion of life when death begins to occupy one's mind. He shouldn't have been surprised. In fact, he wasn't surprised, but he felt smashed and beaten. He had really loved Doris, even if he had forgotten to tell her often enough when she was alive. Without thinking, he had constructed a life in which she would always be near him. Now he was lost, but he was man enough to know he couldn't just curl up and cower until his own time came, so he made the most of what he had.

Most afternoons he spent pursuing his hobby of wood-working. When he retired from the Philadelphia Police Department in the early nineties, he had no hobbies, unless one counts watching television until you fall asleep in your recliner as a hobby. Doris, on the other hand, was very fond of birds and enjoyed going out birding with like-minded friends. Try as he might, he couldn't develop that interest. At the same time, he knew he couldn't spend the rest of his life doing nothing, so when he retired and the couple moved to Virginia's Eastern Shore—where Doris found bird watching to be much more rewarding than in Northeast Philadelphia—he chose wood-working as a pastime. He eventually became rather good at it.

At first he made birdhouses, doghouses, and bookcases, until all his friends and neighbors in Port St. George, and all his relatives back in Pennsport and South Jersey, had at least one of his creations, and he'd saturated the giveaway wood-crafts market. Next, he started restoring the couple's Victorian house on Knight Street, room by room, repairing damaged plaster or moldings and painting them, and even adding corner cabinets, picture rails, and crown moldings. His masterpiece was to have been a new kitchen for Doris for which he would make all the cabinets. He had spared nothing, buying the finest purpleheart from a supplier who claimed to practice sustaina-ble forestry, which meant he paid top dollar, and carefully stacking and covering the wood in his shop to achieve the exact degree of dryness for working. Besides being very expensive, purpleheart required special tools due to its hardness and den-sity, and emitted poisonous chemicals when cut or sanded, but Callahan didn't care. Doris had chosen the wood because she liked the color, and as far as he was concerned that was suffi-cient reason to use it. He had already established a well-equipped shop in the former two-horse stable behind their house. To further prepare for the project, he bought a top qual-ity dust mask and some elegant German saw blades, and he was ready and eager to start. But, when a routine mammogram showed a large abnormality deep in Doris's left breast, he didn't.

Instead, this discovery precipitated three years of doctor's appointments, surgical procedures, radiotherapy and chemo-therapy treatments, hospitalizations, infections, reactions to drugs, consultations, evaluations, re-evaluations, and second, third, and fourth opinions. In the end, none of these mattered, and Callahan was alone for the first time in thirty-eight years.

After months of trying to adjust, he knew what he would do. He didn't want to build a new kitchen for a departed wife—and besides, the psychologist who lived at the end of his street might find that behavior peculiar, and make a sly comment. Instead, on his sixtieth birthday, Callahan selected enough purpleheart from his seasoned stock to build his own coffin. Some people might find that peculiar, too, but he had the wood, he had the tools, and, as Doris's experience had demonstrated, when you've spent six decades on this planet, anything can happen.

Not that he was in any hurry to die. He missed Doris, but he still liked being alive. He had made many good friends since moving to Port St. George, and he found the passing parade of human life in this tiny Eastern Shore town to be very enjoyable. Although he and Doris never had children, he had several nephews and nieces of various ages whom he loved and wanted to see grow to maturity and succeed in life. He enjoyed watching their lives unfolding, and intended to be available to help if needed. So, in constructing his own coffin, he was not signaling a desire for death, but simply recognizing the reality of being sixty years old. Or, to put it another way, as he sometimes did when faced with a concerned query from a friend or relative, "Just because you have a life jacket on your boat doesn't mean you're hoping it will sink."

* * *

A Coffin for Callahan

Before starting to build his coffin, Callahan researched the Virginia law on burials. There was no requirement for any particular type of casket for either burial or cremation, and since he had yet to decide on his preferred method of disposing of his remains, this freedom of choice was gratifying. However, he felt that not having some type of container would be like arriving naked to a wedding. That might be acceptable for some people, but not for Callahan, who definitely wanted be enclosed for his final ceremony. Caskets could be made of practically anything, so his choice of a homemade wooden vessel for his remains was no problem.

His one quibble with the law's wording was the use of the term *casket*. To him a casket sounded frilly and insufficient for holding a man's remains until kingdom come. A casket held jewelry, or maybe the index finger of a martyr. The word casket was effete, although Callahan would never have used that word. In Callahan's opinion, cops aren't buried in caskets. They're buried in coffins.

Finding a set of detailed coffin plans on the Internet took only a few minutes after Mrs. Davis showed him how to turn on his computer and use the browser. Doris had always done everything computer-related in their home, so Callahan inherited a nearly new computer that was about as useful to him as the closet full of Doris's clothes he'd also inherited, and quickly taken to the Food Bank thrift store. Mrs. Davis, always eager to be helpful, had given him computer "lessons," which didn't make much of an impression. So if he needed to do something with the computer, he depended on her for help. He was well aware of the downside. Any favors he obtained from Mrs. Davis must be repaid. He probably could have gotten away without doing so, but that was not his way. He had grown up in a tight-knit, Irish American neighborhood where every favor (or insult) was kept in a mental journal. Balancing these books was one of the ways you earned acceptance in the community and preserved your self-respect. While Callahan felt an obligation to return each of Mrs. Davis's favors, he worried that she might interpret his gestures as more than simple balancing transactions.

Second

Does success really have a sweet smell? Carter Wingate probably would have said so as his shoulder brushed the dense honeysuckle clogging the old woman's garden path. A few words on the shameful plight of the lonely elderly and his earnest insistence that her too-hard, too-dry, flavorless coffee cake was just the way his dear, late mother made it (which was true—he had detested his mother's coffee cake, too), and he'd hooked her. After his generous offer of fifteen hundred dollars in cash for her late husband's shoe box coin collection, "because you remind me of my late Aunt Mary," he was ready to travel. With assurance born of much practice, he mouthed closing pleasantries in his soothing Southern drawl, pled further commitments, and was out the door with a bundle under his arm.

Wingate had already lined up a buyer for the pennies from the 1940s, and knew it would be easy to find someone to take the late 1800s silver dollars. He reckoned he had bagged more than three thousand dollars in profit in less than an hour, simply by chatting up a trusting elderly lady. He enjoyed besting people this way, and he resented his fellow members of the human race for being such pussies that they couldn't take advantage of people the way he did. He hated the people he bested even more because they were such inert lumps of warm flesh that they allowed themselves to be taken. In fact, there was almost nobody Henry Carter Wingate IV liked—other than himself, of course.

He pictured himself as a predator, like a cheetah on the Serengeti, who assists Mother Nature by picking off the weak and the doomed. By tricking gullible people out of their pitiful treasures, he was performing a valuable public service—speeding the financial ruin of suckers who were so stupid they did not deserve to keep on living. If he didn't deprive these fools of their excess assets, they might cash them in at fair market value to buy medicine, their lives might be extended, and the average intelligence of the world's population would decline even more rapidly than it was doing already.

As he walked to his vintage Mercedes (parked well down the block, since he had told the widow he was a retired schoolteacher who only traveled by bus), he remembered that he must buy a new leash for Orion, his faithful white Scottie. He could swing by the mall outside Salisbury, Maryland, pick up the leash in the pet store there, and be home in about an hour. For Carter Wingate, it didn't get much sweeter than this. He was a happy man.

His happiness was hardly accidental. He had earned it. Unlike the host of withering gray morons whom he regularly fleeced to supplement his investment income (and incidentally preserve the world's IQ), Carter Wingate had planned ahead. After several years building his business, he left Nevada and returned to the East, where he eventually set himself up in a historically significant former plantation house overlooking a beautiful creek draining to the Chesapeake Bay. He had furnished the house exquisitely (good taste being one of his many talents) and he had worked tirelessly to bring the garden up to world-class horticultural standards. He kept himself fit, ate very well, but carefully, and drank only the best wines and liquors—never to excess. In short, he had singlehandedly created a world that met nearly all of his needs, and made him happy every day. He was his own god and his own best friend.

Naturally, some of his needs could not be met, even in an exquisite house on St. George Creek. For instance, he enjoyed gambling, and found lotteries and scratch-offs to be boring and stupid, so he had to travel to casinos in various places where he could play poker with people who offered at least some semblance of a challenge. He also enjoyed sex, particularly with strangers, whether male or female. This interest was also better pursued at places distant from home, where his partners were unlikely to be seen again.

Port St. George, the settlement nearest his home, had seen its best days prior to the arrival of the railroad in the late 19th century. Until then it had been a bustling port, shipping shellfish and potatoes to Baltimore, lumber to New York, and Virginia tobacco to the world. When trains started coming to nearby Thistle, the water trade declined, and with the coming of a paved highway and the flight of the town's bigger stores to the edge of the thoroughfare, its fortunes deteriorated further. By the time Carter Wingate discovered the little town, its glory days existed only in the memories of elderly residents. This was not a problem, in Wingate's view, because he was looking for a place that was out of the way, yet had a historic past to give it stature, a genteel appearance, and a quiet lifestyle. He wasn't looking for place that was up and coming so much as one that was down and going, which is to say—easy to hide in.

Third

Bluebirds love to have babies, or so Doris had reminded Callahan many times. In fact, they are so enamored of the experience of having tiny chicks to feed for days on end that they sometimes produce more than one clutch of penny-sized blue eggs in a season. This fact made little impression on Callahan until the spring after Doris died. The bluebirds she had observed so faithfully came back as always to nest in the box he had made for them, but Doris wasn't there to watch and worry. Suddenly, Callahan found himself fretting over the birds. Were they safe? Were they laying eggs? Were they finding enough food for their young?

Having seen a brood through to maturity in April and May, he was now beginning to wonder if they were going to have a second family. They had done so three years ago in a particularly mild summer. Nothing Callahan had ever done for Doris seemed to thrill her as much as seeing those birds mate a second time and raise another brood. Callahan became the keeper of the flame. Every other day or so he would walk down to the creek edge and sit quietly on a bench he had made for Doris. After a few minutes the bluebirds would forget he was there and go about their business. Today he sat patiently, coffee cup in hand, seeking to discover how the mating was progressing. The bluebirds were still in the area, and they seemed to be adding bits of grass and pine shatters to the nest, but they were not bringing food. That meant they were expecting, but had no babies to care for yet. He would have to return the next day and check again.

A Coffin for Callahan

When he returned to his house, Callahan put his coffee mug in the dishwasher, and was beginning to think about what he could get done in the wood shop before it became uncomfortably warm, when he heard a rapping at the door. "Good morning, Edward," said Mrs. Davis, standing outside the screen door. She held a plate of freshly baked corn muffins. "I couldn't resist the urge to bake this morning, and made too many for only little me."

"As always, you're too kind, Eileen," said Callahan as he opened the screen door. He had been aware for some time that Mrs. Davis often made too much food for herself and then decided that Callahan needed to eat the excess. It was as if she feared he couldn't feed himself without a woman in the house, and was determined to correct both shortcomings at once. (Or, as she would have phrased it, "To kill two birds with one stone.")

"The only way to have a friend is to be one," she replied.

"Who said that?"

"Emerson. Or, maybe it was Walt Whitman. I'm not sure. I'll have to look it up. Anyway, it's certainly true."

"Right you are. Care for a coffee?"

"Thanks, but I can't stay." Mrs. Davis almost always said she couldn't stay, but then lingered, sometimes for hours. "Well, okay, maybe a short one."

Callahan poured the coffee and buttered one of the still warm corn muffins. They were delicious—far better than he or Doris could make—but he tried not to encourage Mrs. Davis too much, or she would cook every meal for him. "So what's on your calendar for today?"

"I'm going to church later to help a group of our ladies clean the kitchen. We're going to do the ovens, pull everything out and clean behind, and even wash the windows."

"Sounds like quite a project."

"Many hands make light work," said Mrs. Davis, as she topped up her coffee. "How about you?"

"I was going to cut out some of my coffin parts."

"Oh, Edward, I wish you would drop that. It's so dreary. You're still a young man. You shouldn't be wasting your time on a coffin—at least not for many years. You're fit, and very strong and healthy. You could be out fishing, or reading, or taking up a hobby."

"I have a hobby. Woodworking."

"Of course, and that's a fine hobby, but you're building the wrong thing. You should volunteer for Habitat for Humanity. Building houses for deserving folks is much more positive than coffin building."

"I've also taken up bird watching."

"Like Doris?"

"Not so much like her as in her place. I'm making a point to watch the bluebirds, to be sure they're all right."

"That's wonderful. A life without birds is like meat without seasoning."

"I do what I can." He drained his coffee cup and picked up his plate. "You'll have to excuse me Eileen, but I really do need to cut out the pieces for my coffin this morning."

Mrs. Davis frowned. "You know what they say, 'Don't put off till tomorrow what you can do today.' However, if you want my opinion, which I imagine you don't, I really believe you are too young, healthy, and handsome a man to be working on such a dreadful thing."

"Thanks for the corn muffins." Callahan opened the screen door and held it as she went out.

Once in his shop, Callahan reviewed the cut list. He was trying to decide what would be the most efficient way to begin when he found himself thinking about Doris instead. He sat down on a stool he kept for occasionally resting his legs in the shop. He still missed her terribly. Every so often this happened. He would have a fleeting memory of Doris, and the energy would go out of him. He would then feel a need to sit a while doing nothing.

She had been a quiet woman. It's a favorite complaint of men that women chatter all the time—usually about things of no consequence (at least in the opinion of the men). Whether that characterization is true or not, it certainly didn't apply to Doris. If something needed to be said, she said it, but the rest of the time she kept her own counsel. Sometimes Callahan wondered what she was thinking when she was so quiet, and occasionally he would ask. Her replies were usually vague and noncommittal, "Nothing much" or "Whether we should have the leftover ham tonight" or "Just daydreaming."

Despite these denials, he knew she was doing real thinking, because whenever there was a problem to be solved, she would listen to his worries and ideas for solutions, and then, often after a day or two of thought, would present her own version— almost always a better idea. Again and again he would be amazed at how elegantly her idea solved a problem that to him had seemed intractable. But he could never call up the courage to ask her to think about the one problem that troubled him most, the one that had changed both their lives forever. And now it was too late.

Fourth

Leaving behind the nation's capital and his latest victim (many of his suckers were widows of government workers, so Wingate visited the Washington, D.C. area often), he noticed that it was too late in the afternoon to drive legally on U.S. 50 in the HOV lane. He always drove legal speeds and followed the traffic rules. This was not from any particular respect for society's laws, but because he didn't like to put himself in a position where a police officer had an excuse to ask him questions. Fortunately, as if further proof were needed that this was Carter Wingate's lucky day, he saw, standing by the side of the road next to two backpacks and a large water bottle, a young woman—slender, blonde, and vulnerable. He pulled over. "Hello, darling. Where to?"

"I need to go to Salisbury."

"So do I. Hop in."

Becky was studying early childhood education at Salisbury University. She and her boyfriend had been visiting the boy's parents in the Maryland suburbs of D.C. when the couple had a serious fight and she walked out. Too proud and angry to admit she didn't have enough money for bus fare back to college, she took the local suburban train system to the end of the line, and was hitchhiking the remaining hundred and ten miles. Carter Wingate congratulated himself on his ability to detect that she was in trouble from a quick glance at her face.

"Your troubles are over, Becky," he said, prolonging his gaze long enough to enjoy the way her small firm breasts filled out her sweat-stained tank top. He told her his name was Chuck Wood, and smiled when she didn't seem to get the joke.

With his pretty passenger, not only would he be able to drive legally in the HOV lane and thereby save some time on the highway, but he might be able to conjure a little bonus fun for himself along the way.

The pair chatted amiably as they drove to the end of the HOV lane, and then continued over the Bay Bridge to the Eastern Shore of Maryland. As a little hint about his thinking, Wingate mentioned in passing that some people considered him to be a libertine. Becky misunderstood and asked him if he agreed with the Libertarian Party's position on use of marijuana and other mind-altering drugs. Wingate tittered at her naiveté, and in a straightforward confession of his philosophy of life said he believed people should be allowed to do what they felt like whenever they felt like doing it.

About an hour into the journey, it had started to rain heavily, with occasional thunder and lightning. Wingate felt this was one more way that events were unfolding in his favor, and made his proposition. He would pull off the road into a little roadside park he knew was coming up soon, and Becky would pay her fare for the ride—a little sexual service for her driver— or else her ride would be over. She wouldn't even have to take any of her clothes off, he said, unless she wanted to, of course, just put her pretty face down between his chest and the steering wheel, open her mouth, and do him a quick favor. She didn't take any clothes off, and she didn't pay the fare either. Wingate left her on the side of the road in the rain, looking thinner, less blonde, and more vulnerable than ever.

* * *

After picking up a new leash for Orion, Wingate began to think about dinner. He would be in Port St. George in a little over an hour, and it was his custom to reward himself after a successful trip. Although he had taught himself to cook at a level that, in his opinion, exceeded the performance of most of the Cordon Bleu chefs whose restaurants he had visited, he enjoyed a lazy evening once in a while—especially if he had done well at someone else's expense. As he drove slowly down Main Street, he recalled that Duck's Store Restaurant had a new chef. When he did eat out, Wingate's usual local dining spot was Mario's, a small restaurant run by an artist who came to Port St. George from Argentina via New York City many years ago. The entrée selection was eclectic and very creative, and the place had an excellent, reasonably priced wine list. Its interior was dark, and the tables were fairly far apart so that interaction with other diners was unlikely, an ideal arrangement for the limelight-avoiding Carter Wingate.

However, the new chef at Duck's Store might be somebody special, so Wingate decided to vary his routine. In that objective, he succeeded beyond anything he could have imagined.

Fifth

Recalling that episode in his past was not what Callahan wanted. Seeking a distraction, despite the closeness to lunchtime, he walked over to the Main Street Bakery. The early morning crowd had left. There were only a couple of people in the shop, and he didn't know either of them, so he bought his usual coffee and chocolate chip cookie and settled down to read the paper alone. It was not long before he was interrupted.

"Good morning, Mr. Callahan," said Delbert Dix, a recent college graduate who occasionally stopped in the bakery for a morning coffee break. Callahan enjoyed chatting with the younger man because he represented a change from discussions of the Redskins, the Orioles, the Ravens, or events that happened on the Eastern Shore forty years ago.

"Hey, Delbert, how are things?"

"Very well, sir, very well, indeed. After far too much fuss and bother, I've finally settled on a topic for my book, and I've been doing research for about a week in my off hours." A graduate of the University of Virginia with a degree in American Studies, Delbert had written a thesis on farming in the Shenandoah Valley during the Great Depression. A shortened version had been published and won an award. Unfortunately, this early success did not lead to a paying job, so he returned home to work for his uncle driving a propane delivery truck. He lived with his mother, and was trying to keep his education fresh by writing a book in his spare time.

"So what's your topic?"

"Murders of the Eastern Shore."

"Should be an easy book to write, as few murders as there are here compared to Philadelphia or Chicago."

"Not so! Well, of course, we don't have as many murders as the big cities do, but you'd be amazed how many grisly murders there have been here over the years. Right now, Virginia is about in the middle of the pack of U.S states, with 6.1 murders per 100,000 people."

"How does the Eastern Shore compare?"

"It's hard to say, because we have such a small population. For the most recent year, we had only two murders, which works out to a rate of about 6 per 100,000, which, although it seems to be about the same as the state, is not really statistically valid. Some years we don't have any murders here."

"So what's a typical Eastern Shore murder like?"

"How about this one?" Delbert sat up straight in his chair. "In 1922 a storekeeper down near Wachapreague was beaten on the head with a cart axle and died. Soon afterward, they arrested the couple that lived in the apartment over the store."

"Why?"

"Although they claimed to be asleep when it happened, bloodhounds found a trail from the scene of the crime straight up to their apartment, and investigators later found bloody clothing of both of them hidden under the apartment floorboards. Also, the guy had been charged with murder before, and he'd recently been in jail for making moonshine."

"Motive?"

"The county prosecutor claimed that the storekeeper and the accused had been in business together, making whiskey with a still they kept on the third floor of the store. While his partner was in jail on Prohibition violations, the storekeeper supposedly sold three barrels of whiskey they had made, and the theory was that he refused to pay his partner a share of the proceeds."

"And the couple was convicted?"

"Amazingly, no. They claimed that someone came to the store about eleven o'clock that night and knocked on the door, it being the usual thing for customers to come at all hours."

"Especially if you're selling moonshine."

"Right, so the story was that, when a second customer came later, at around midnight, and woke everybody up again, they found the storekeeper almost dead, sitting in the store and mumbling. He never said anything clear enough to point to his murderer, and later he died."

"So they found this first customer and arrested him?"

"No, they just let the couple off, because they assumed the first customer was the perpetrator—although they did serve time for making whiskey."

"You mean the court took the word of a bootlegging criminal who'd been previously charged with murder, that this other customer, the supposed true murderer that nobody ever saw and they never found, had come to the store and killed its owner?"

"Exactly."

"What about physical evidence."

"They took fingerprints off the murder weapon, but there were so many prints they decided none of them were of any use. The fingerprints of the man from the upstairs apartment were on the axle because he handled it in the presence of the prosecuting attorney during the investigation."

"Damn! That's clever."

"He was a former cop."

Callahan slowly smiled. "Figures."

"Actually, Mr. Callahan, that one was atypical because of the method. Clubs or blunt instruments were used rarely. Shooting was by far the most popular. Forty-nine out of the hundred and fourteen I've researched so far involved a firearm. A lot of the causes of death are unknown, but the second most popular of the known methods was stabbing, followed by beatings or fistfights, clubs or other blunt instruments, and then drowning. Two involved an axe, two poison, one strangling, and one bomb."

"A bomb?"

"Yeah, a mail bomb."

"You'll have to tell me about that one someday, but now I should be getting back for lunch if I'm going to accomplish anything today. Watch yourself around all those murderers, Delbert."

* * *

After a minimal lunch, Callahan took his coffee and headed down to his bench near the creek. Soon the bluebirds began to ignore him. The female was nowhere to be seen, but the male was busy visiting the bluebird house, and then going out foraging for nesting straws or food. Callahan decided the female must be laying, or perhaps had already laid her eggs. He was surprised at how much satisfaction this knowledge of avian reproduction gave him. Was this what Doris experienced with these birds? he wondered. If so, it was easy to see how she became so attached to them. He almost gave in to the temptation to open the hatch on the bluebird house roof and peek in. Amazingly, the birds normally don't mind such intrusions, and a look-see would confirm his supposition. Then he started worrying he might upset them, so he decided to put off checking until tomorrow.

Next his mind turned to coffins. He had been reading about them and had learned a few things. The word was first used in the English language in 1380 according to one source and 1525 according to another. Either way, a coffin was an old concept, which appealed to Callahan. He wouldn't want to be buried in something modern. That didn't seem to fit with the concept of death as an eternal experience.

Naturally, the English word coffin came originally from Latin—cophinus—which means basket, via the early French cophin, which in French has since morphed into couffin, which no longer means basket, but bassinet. So I guess you start out as a basket case and you end up as one, thought Callahan with a smile when he read this. The ancient Egyptians placed mummies in stone sarcophagi. The word literally means "flesh eaters." Callahan got a kick out of that one also. The Bible mentions only one person who used a coffin, which surprised him, considering how often death occurs in that book. The deceased was Joseph, but he died in Egypt, where coffins were the fashion at the time. Had he died in Jerusalem, he would have been stuck in a cave and allowed to decay to bones. After a year or so his family would come and collect the bones and put them in a bone box. For reasons he could not explain, Callahan was repelled by the idea of someone handling his bones after he had been laid to rest. If he were dead and had decayed to a skeleton, he certainly wouldn't feel anything, but the thought still made him squirm. Eternal rest means eternal rest, he thought, frowning.

Sixth

Duck's Store Restaurant occupied the building of a former general store. Many years after the closing of the store, which had been a hub of waterfront commerce for nearly a century and a half, new owners moved the building to a location nearer to the town wharf. Buildings on the Eastern Shore were often picked up and moved—some more than once—so the act of moving in itself was not remarkable. Rumor has it that the old store was moved to its present location to block the creek view of the person who lived in a nearby house. Duck's was only the most recent of several restaurants that operated in the old store building with varying degrees of success as owners and chefs came and went.

At his request, Carter Wingate was seated at a table along one wall where no one could get behind him and he could see the dining room door. For many years, he had followed this practice. Like a gunslinger in a western movie, he preferred being able to cover his back and see who was coming in. It gave him a feeling of control of the situation, which he found satisfying. As he waited for his order of craft beer and an appetizer of mini crab cakes on homemade tortilla chips, he surveyed the restaurant. It didn't seem very busy, but it was early yet. While he did not know the new chef, he hoped the guy would succeed, so as to increase the number of places in Port St. George where one could enjoy a truly fine meal. At the same time, he hoped the new chef wouldn't succeed too well, because Wingate disliked crowds.

On this particular Wednesday evening, there were two young couples at the bar wearing jeans and T-shirts with brand names prominently displayed. These were likely local people, he thought, because their clothes looked cheaply made and well worn. There also was a party of four in one corner consisting of an older couple and a younger couple—probably someone from the Eastern Shore returning home with a new friend to introduce to the parents. The only other diner was a woman sitting alone near a window. She had a glass of white wine in front of her and appeared to be waiting for her first course. She was looking out at the creek, a sure sign she was a tourist. Locals had seen enough creek views to last a lifetime, so they usually looked at their food or their phones—eager for interesting news and indifferent to the nature outside.

The woman, looked vaguely familiar to Wingate, but he couldn't place her. He took a moment from scanning the menu to scan the woman. He liked what he saw. She was well dressed in a classic way, with slacks that flattered her well-formed legs and a white, sleeveless blouse with a mildly scooped neckline. Although she appeared to be close to his own age, she was still a looker. He would have liked it if her hair were a little longer, but he accepted the fact that when women hit forty most of them start shortening their hair. This lady looked as if she might be exactly what he needed after his misfire with young Becky. He would let her enjoy her meal, and when she finished, and perhaps was wondering what to do next in a quiet little town, he would make his move.

Seventh

The cut list Callahan had obtained for his coffin showed twenty-seven parts—four side pieces, a head board, a toe board, a top, a floor, and a variety of ribs and rails to aid the alignment and fastening of the other pieces. Due to one distraction or another, he had made little progress cutting out these parts. In fact, he had done only the rails, a simple one-inch by two-inch ripping job on the table saw, and even these pieces he had not yet cut to length. He felt like a slacker.

Perhaps his lack of focus stemmed from nagging doubts regarding the size of the coffin in the generic plan he was following. The widest part looked too small. The plans called for a twenty-four inch maximum width where Callahan's shoulders would be. If he put a padded lining in the coffin, it would become narrower. If they dressed him in a suit for burial, his broad shoulders would be widened further. He had only one piece of purpleheart wider than twenty-four inches, and he wanted a one-piece lid, so there was no margin for error. He had to measure his shoulders before going further.

To make the measurement while working alone, he tied a large wooden block to a string about four feet long. Next, he passed the free end of the string around the leg of his saw table and lay on his back on the floor with his right shoulder pressed against the table leg. His plan was to pull on the string until he felt the pressure of the wood block on his left shoulder, sit up carefully so as not to disturb the block, and then use a tape measure to obtain the distance from the block to the table leg. He had pulled the string until he could feel the wood block pressed firmly against his shoulder, and was about to get up and take the measurement when Mrs. Davis burst into the workshop and shrieked, "Edward!" in a high-pitched, airy voice he had never heard from her before. She knelt beside him and put her hand on his heart. "Are you all right?"

"I'm fine," he said, sitting up as quickly as he could. "There's nothing wrong with me that wasn't already wrong. I was just measuring across my shoulders."

"Lordy, lordy, you frightened me so." She brushed back her thin salt and pepper hair. "I thought you had gone straight into the hereafter like my dear Preston Lee."

"I'm only preparing to go, Eileen. Not gone yet."

"You should have asked me to help." She grabbed the tape measure off the bench. "Stand up."

"It's better if I'm lying down and relaxed, as if I'm dead."

"What's better?"

"The measurement. If I'm lying down and relaxed, my shoulder width will be closer to what it'll be when I'm a stiff."

Mrs. Davis grimaced and rolled her eyes, but she dutifully pulled out the metal tape and held it flat on the floor so Callahan could lie on it. She pressed her hand against his shoulder, and then read out the measurement—"twenty-nine and a half inches."

Callahan rose and dusted himself off. "Thank you, Eileen," he said. As he spoke he wondered what he would owe Mrs. Davis for her assistance. The answer would not be long coming.

After his neighbor had left for home, Callahan measured from the wood block to table leg distance to confirm her measurement, found the same result, and recorded "29½" on a piece of scrap wood. Next he cleaned up the shop and went to his house for some iced tea. He took his glass to the side porch and sat in silence. He thought about bluebirds and their babies. He thought about himself and Doris, and the babies they never had. Would he have really enjoyed having children, or would he have simply worried himself to death? Whenever he saw a young person these days, whether it was a young woman jogging behind a three-wheeled baby stroller in the middle of Duke Street or Delbert with his unwritten book of murders and dead-end job, his natural inclination was to worry about them.

At least the kids he worried about have jobs and are trying to make something of themselves. What about all the others? Parents are so cautious these days, keeping kids away from peanut butter, contact sports, and sex flicks, only to watch helplessly when they become young adults and proceed to ingest psychoactive substances of unknown composition purchased from criminals. Government officials at all levels say they can't afford to give kids an education, but when a young person commits a minor crime, money is always found to lock them up. What a world we live in!

* * *

It took Callahan a couple of hours to redraw his set of coffin plans to account for a lid wide enough for his shoulders. The end and side pieces had changed little, but the top and bottom pieces had to be widened considerably and the bevels on the vertical braces had to have different angles—slightly narrower at the shoulders and slightly wider at the head and toe. Having set up the ripping angle for the head and toe pieces on his table saw, he decided that now was a good time for coffee and a cookie. Normally he treated himself only in the mornings, but much experience with woodworking had shown him that stupid mistakes usually occur when cuts are made too soon after setting them up. A little reflection on the work to be done often reveals an error in thinking. He would go to the bakery and reflect over coffee. As Mrs. Davis would say (if she hadn't done so already) "measure twice, cut once."

On the way to the bakery Callahan recalled a story his uncle Jack O'Leary told him about coffin making in Ireland. As a youth Jack had worked in a furniture shop that made coffins as a sideline. One day he and his mates hurriedly built a coffin for an elderly lady who had died unexpectedly. There was a mix-up about who was deceased, Mrs. Kelly who was short or Miss Grogan who was tall. When Miss Grogan was placed inside, her knees stuck up so the lid could not be closed. Jack and the undertaker and the fat boy who worked at the pub sat down hard on the lid a few times until the old lady's legs broke and they could nail the coffin shut. Callahan made a mental note to double-check the length of his coffin against his height before he cut anything.

When he arrived at the bakery, he was surprised to find Delbert Dix, also taking an unusual break. He asked why.

"I got stuck in my writing, and needed some time away. This is my day off, so I thought I could write all day and make some real progress. Writing continuously is a lot harder than driving a propane truck continuously. I needed a break."

"Me too. How's your project coming?"

"Pretty well, really, despite today's experience. But there are so many different murder stories. I'm having trouble figuring out how to arrange them—chronologically, by motive, by method, by some characteristic of the murderer or his victim—I'm floundering."

"Motive wouldn't be good."

"Why not?"

"Because it's often unknown, even to the murderer himself."

"Lots of the ones on the Shore seem to involve a combination of grudges, guns, and booze."

"Proves the Eastern Shore isn't so different from the rest of the world after all."

"Some things are quite different. Let me tell you an unusual one and see what you think. This one happened just north of here in Maryland, so it's out of my book's scope, but it's interesting. There was this girl named Laura Fincham, who thought she was a man."

"Not that unusual."

"This was in 1876. There was this other girl, named Miss Horn, whom Fincham thought was becoming too interested in someone else."

"Man or woman?"

"The paper didn't say. Another man, I suppose—well—of course Miss Fincham was not really a man, but you know what I mean. Anyhow, Miss Fincham shot and killed Miss Horn."

"How'd she make out at trial?"

"Acquitted. Insanity."

"She'd never get off on that one today."

Eighth

The new chef's menu was indeed interesting, and Wingate selected a chilled cherry soup, garden salad, and broiled lobster tail. He chose an Australian Sauvignon Blanc to try, and all was golden. He savored the satisfaction of his very successful trip, with a delicious meal as his well-deserved reward.

When his salad arrived, Wingate glanced in the direction of the woman at the window. As the setting sun hit her face, he was reminded of woman he had known many years ago, who, like most good-looking women, he had wanted to take to bed. In a rare example of his failing to achieve one of his desires, he had moved away not long after the woman's husband was sent to prison. The absence of the husband would have created an ideal situation for him to pursue his objective, but there were complications that made it impossible. He regretted the loss.

About twenty minutes later, as Wingate finished his entrée, he noticed that the woman at the window was having her coffee. He declined dessert and coffee, left cash on his table for his check and a modest tip, and strolled to her table. "Please forgive me for being so forward, ma'am, but I noticed you are alone and look like a visitor. May I offer you a leisurely guided tour of our charming little town?"

The woman looked up, obviously shaken from her thoughts. She looked him over briefly, and then frowned. "Hello, Charlie," she said.

"You must be mistaken, ma'am. My name is not Charlie," he said in his most mellifluous Georgian accent. "I'm Carter Wingate IV, and most pleased to meet you Miss . . . ."

"*Mrs.*—Hazel Jones, Charlie. You may not remember me, but I've never forgotten you."

The raising of her voice confirmed it. This was indeed the woman Wingate had known in his previous life, which he had spent a lot of time and money trying to escape. Now he was standing in front of the most dangerous person from that past life. He had told her his name, and he had stated that he lived locally. While he tried to conceive an escape plan, he covered his anxiety with words. "Of course, Hazel, forgive me for not recognizing you at first. What a pleasure it is to see you again!"

"Tell me something I'll believe, like why you sent my Robert to prison."

"Robert did not defend himself. That's why he went to prison."

"You lied about seeing him at the plant. Without your testimony, he would be free."

"I know you never believed my testimony, but if Robert had an alibi, why didn't he use it? His failure to speak up sealed his fate."

"Please leave. Now."

"Hazel, let's be reasonable. We're old friends. Can't we enjoy our time together without fighting over ancient history?"

"It's not ancient history to me. My husband is still in prison for a murder he did not commit."

Lies came easily to Carter Wingate, especially when he felt under pressure. "Perhaps we could work together to free him. You're probably unaware of this, but since I got out of the plastics business, I've taken a law degree. I have legal connections throughout the South, and I'm sure my influence would matter. Working together, we could get Robert out on parole, or possibly even a commutation of his sentence."

"You've always been a bullshitter, Charlie. Don't waste my time."

"Hazel, really, you are missing a golden opportunity. I've always cared for you and don't want to see you suffer any longer."

"I asked you to leave. Waiter!"

The waiter arrived and before Hazel Jones could open her mouth, Wingate ordered coffee for himself. He sat down at her table. "Please, Hazel, hear me out. Then, if you continue to feel as you do now, I will go quietly and trouble you no more."

"Let's get it over with." Hazel Jones listened as Wingate used his persuasive skills to the utmost, but after ten minutes of him spinning every pie-in-the-sky story he could think of, she got up to leave, and promptly sat back in her chair. "I feel dizzy."

"It's my fault. I've upset you by bringing up these old, bad memories. I apologize unreservedly. May I walk you to your car?"

Reluctantly, Hazel Jones held Wingate's arm as he paid her bill in cash and led her from the restaurant dining room to the parking lot. While the lady on his arm became increasingly disoriented and unsteady on her feet, Wingate moved with confidence. One quick flip of his antique locket ring over her coffee cup when she glanced momentarily toward the sunset over the creek, and he had regained control. The tiny pill that dropped into her cup did exactly what it had done to so many unsuspecting females before her.

Ninth

Callahan munched the last of his cookie. "I guess that kind of murder doesn't happen often here, maybe anywhere."

"Actually, there was an attempted murder in 1888 in Craddockville that was kind of similar. A tailor, named Andrew Brucie, thought he was a woman. As a prank, a young fellow named John Kimball pretended to be in love with him. To keep the prank going, Kimball proposed to Brucie, who accepted, and they set a wedding date.

"Brucie took the proposal very seriously and dropped everything to prepare for the wedding and the big feast he planned to have. According to the newspaper story, the two of them were on their way home from a neighbor's house when they began to argue about the color of the wedding dress. Brucie wanted bright red. Kimball disagreed, but the newspaper article didn't say what color he wanted. Finally, Kimball brandished his gun, telling Brucie he would shoot him if he didn't change his mind about the dress color. Brucie pulled his own gun, and shot Kimball in the hand and arm, so Kimball returned fire and hit Brucie in the leg and back. They tried to hide what they'd done, but Brucie bled so much they had to confess and they were both arrested."

"Did they get jail time?"

"I don't know. The paper only said they went to court, but didn't give an outcome."

* * *

The next morning, Callahan made a quick check of blue-birds, and this time he opened the lid on the nest box and saw the mother bluebird placidly sitting on the nest. He could see two small blue eggs, and he suspected there were more. He went for his morning coffee and cookie feeling like a proud father.

Delbert Dix was already in the bakery, reading the newspaper. "Another writing day gone bad?" asked Callahan.

"Excellent guess. The propane truck's in the shop, so I took another day off, believing it would be a perfect opportunity to write some more, but my muse is taking a snooze. There's so much information and some of the deaths seem so pointless. And some of them may not even be murders anyway. I feel overwhelmed. Consider this example. There was this man named William Joiner, who died in his own home, near Savageville, of pneumonia. He caught the pneumonia because his ribs were broken as a result of a fight over a game of dominoes."

"Dominoes?"

"That's right. He was playing dominoes in a bar with a guy named Edward Mann. Believing he was entitled to a dollar, which he thought was their bet on the game, Mr. Joiner accused Mr. Mann of cheating when he refused to give him the dollar. In the fight that followed, Mann pushed Joiner, who tripped over a spittoon and broke several ribs when he hit the floor. Shortly after the fight, he developed pneumonia and died. Was that a murder or not?"

"I'm a former cop, not a lawyer, but I'd say it would be manslaughter or negligent homicide, but not murder one. What did the jury say?"

"That's one of my biggest frustrations. For so many of these stories there's no follow-up in the papers. They say somebody is scheduled to appear before the grand jury or has a court date or whatever, but then there's no mention of the outcome in later editions."

"Stories that leave *you* hanging—instead of the murderer."

"Exactly, but fortunately they're not all like that. Let me tell you one with a conclusion. One night three guys went to the house of a man named William Black in Daugherty. When he answered the door, one of the men lit a match for some light, and another man, named Robert Sherman, shot Mr. Black dead. Apparently the reason was that Black had implicated Sherman for stealing a harness several months before. To avoid prosecution on that charge, Sherman had jumped bail and fled to Baltimore. He came back the night of the murder, and arrived on the 9 o'clock train. He went immediately to Black's house and shot him.

"His plan was to return to Baltimore on the midnight train from Keller, but he was late reaching the station, missed the train, and was captured. Sherman received a life term, and his two accomplices got twenty years each. Their sentences were the harshest given in the Accomack Circuit Court in two decades."

Having finishing his coffee and cookie, Callahan left Delbert at the bakery and went to the post office for some stamps. He returned to his workshop and, before he did anything else, checked the coffin plans to confirm that there was room for his six-foot-one frame. Reassured, he donned his face mask and goggles and completed the bevel cuts for the head braces in a couple of minutes. Next he used his compound miter saw to carefully cut each of the pieces to length. Inspired, he reset the angle on the table saw for the toe braces and experienced pure joy as he watched the bright colored surfaces emerge. With ease he also set and cut the third angle to make the shoulder braces. He marked each of the pieces he made according to what part it was and set them aside. Recognizing, as Mrs. Davis had told him any number of times, that "pride goeth before the fall," he cleaned up the shop and went into his house for lunch.

Tenth

"Which one is your car, Hazel?"

"Blue. South Carolina plates."

"The little Chevy in the corner of the lot?"

"I feel sick Charlie. I think I'm going to throw up."

"I'm sure you'll feel better in a few minutes."

"No. I'm going to be sick. I can't drive."

"Would you like me to give you a ride somewhere?"

"I don't know. I'm sick."

Wingate unlocked his car and opened the passenger side door. "Here, Hazel, sit in my car for a few minutes. Your troubles will soon be over." He closed the door and went around to the driver's side and got in. "Want to see something fun?"

"Charlie. I'm sick. Everything around me is spinning. Please call an ambulance."

"Look at this Hazel. It's the new leash I bought for Orion. He's my dear little Scottie—white as snow and bright as a button. You'd love him."

"Please. Help me, Charlie."

Carter Wingate took the plastic wrapper off the bright red leather leash. "Isn't this pretty? It's very strong, and a cheerful color that will look great on Orion. And, it has that unmistakable, wonderful feel of real leather. Let me wrap it around your neck and show you." He gently wrapped the leather twice around Hazel Jones's neck.

"Please, Charlie, I'm sick. My head is going round and round. Help me."

"Doesn't that leather feel nice? Do you think Orion will like it?" There was no reply, so he continued. "It's even nicer when it's tighter." Wingate leaned toward her face as if about to kiss her, and then yanked with all his might on the two free ends. "Don't you agree?"

Hazel Jones tried to raise her arms toward her neck, but could lift them only a few inches above her lap before her strength failed and they fell back. After about three minutes of embracing her as if she were his lover, while holding the leash tight, Wingate started the car and drove out of the parking lot. Taking care to drive well below the legal limit, he went down Main Street to Hill Street, and turned toward home.

* * *

Orion barked happily in his run as he saw the car approach. Wingate went to the edge of the fenced run and patted his little friend on the head. He didn't let him out right away, to Orion's dismay, but instead went to his garage and found a hand truck he used occasionally for moving furniture. He placed a kitchen chair on it and went to his car. He dragged the lifeless body of Hazel Jones onto the chair and then, holding her by one shoulder, expertly wheeled her into the garage. He went back for the leash and her purse, locked his car, and let Orion out of his run.

The dog dashed into the garage and sniffed cautiously around Hazel Jones's lifeless body, and then went and sat in a corner. Wingate offered him a treat, but he didn't take it. Instead, he looked at it, sniffed it, and went back to the corner. "Well, then, be a party pooper if you want to," his owner said. "I have work to do anyway."

A Coffin for Callahan

Carter Wingate undressed the body, carefully putting her clothes, shoes, purse, and glasses into a plastic bag. He went to Orion and offered him a sniff of his new leash. The Scottie cowered and whined, so Carter Wingate put the leash into the bag with the other items and put the bundle into his freezer underneath several packages of fish he had caught earlier in the year. He looked at Hazel Jones. Even dead, she's a nice looking woman, he thought. He felt her skin and it was cold on the surface, but as he held his hand still for a few seconds her body felt warm. What the hell, he thought, and went to his bedroom, undressed, and returned in his bathrobe wearing a condom. He spread the limp thighs of Hazel Jones and enjoyed himself with her body. No complaints in the morning from this one, he thought, and smiled. Orion stayed in the corner.

Wingate went and made himself an instant iced tea. He put on black jeans and a dark green T-shirt and found a dark colored sheet. Carefully, he covered the body with the sheet and then wrapped a couple of bungee cords around it to make sure the sheet stayed on. He then wheeled the body out of the garage and down the path across his lawn to the dock. In his shed he found a length of old nylon anchor rope and a concrete block. He slid the body of Hazel Jones off the chair and into his 19-foot Boston Whaler. Orion, usually eager for a boat ride, stayed in the garage.

After binding her ankles together, he tied the free end of the rope to the concrete block and carefully arranged the sheet over her body. He reflected on how his luck seemed boundless. He had passed no cars on the ride home from Port St. George, the night was cloudy, and his nearest neighbor was away that night—a hat trick for someone wanting to take a nocturnal cruise without being observed. Even his bright white, usually barking, dog had decided to sulk. It was as if all the stars had aligned to make everything ideal for pushing Hazel Jones out of his life forever. He couldn't help smiling as he started the outboard.

Eleventh

After a hurried lunch, Callahan headed for the workshop. His work had been going well, and he didn't want to break the streak. As he arranged the pieces with their pencil-drawn cut lines, he realized that one of the reasons he liked woodworking was simply the shop itself. It was a manly place—quiet, no windows, and populated only by clever gadgetry—a terrific place to be alone with one's thoughts. It didn't really matter if one had no thoughts. It was still a good place.

Callahan carefully arranged the pieces in reverse order of size. Because the coffin had six sides—head, toe, two long sides, and two short sides—the larger pieces would not have square corners and would need to be free-handed on the table saw. He would start with the smaller pieces and work his way up in size to minimize the chance of spoiling a piece during this delicate and slightly dangerous operation. Not the least of his concerns was that the lid, which would be made from a single piece of purpleheart almost three feet wide and seven feet long, weighed more than eighty pounds before cutting. Wrestling this single-handedly without spoiling the straight line of the cut would be quite a challenge. Callahan thought of calling on one of his neighbors for help, but decided the presence of a helper would spoil the solitude, which at this moment he was enjoying.

To minimize the chance of mistakes, he cut all the pieces slightly oversize on the first pass. Next he carefully set the six and half degree angle for the toe piece and made the final cut. He set an angle of twenty-two degrees and then did the head piece. He then moved on to the two short sides, the two long sides, and the two boards that together would form the bottom. Finally, he carefully cut out the top. No mistakes! He was thrilled.

As before, he decided to "quit while I'm ahead," as he imagined Mrs. Davis would tell him to do. He picked up all the wood scraps, vacuumed the floor, and piled his finished coffin pieces neatly on the bench.

As he walked back toward the house, he heard "Yoo hoo! Edward! I have news." Mrs. Davis was standing on the sidewalk shouting, so he couldn't avoid her.

"What's up, Eileen?"

"Did you hear about the incident at the town wharf this morning?"

"Nope."

"Some lady from South Carolina went off and left her car next to Duck's."

"Really?"

"Well, she never came back. She just locked her car up and went away. It sat there all night, and all-night parking is not allowed, because of the tides. Chief Watson told me they think maybe she jumped in the creek. She left her car in a two-hour spot and it's been there for more than *twelve hours.*"

"Did they give her a ticket?" Callahan had little confidence in the Port St. George police, who, rather than simply doing their jobs, seemed to enjoy making each minor incident into a grand drama. In Philadelphia, you wrote the ticket and moved on. If the car was still there on your next shift, you called the tow squad.

"They couldn't give her a ticket because they couldn't find her."

"Why didn't they just put the ticket on the windshield for her to find when she returns to her car?"

"I don't know."

"Maybe she's staying in town and had a few too many at Duck's and decided to walk back to her B&B and retrieve her car in the morning. Could be that simple."

"But it's still there, and it's now almost eleven o'clock."

"Maybe she's sleeping in, or enjoying one of Mrs. Nocera's breakfasts."

"Mrs. Nocera's breakfasts are not good for you."

"The only time I had one I thought it was splendid." Callahan and Doris had stayed in Mrs. Nocera's B&B once years ago while they were looking for a house to buy on the Eastern Shore. The place was luxurious, but Doris thought it too expensive, so they started staying at motel in nearby Olden.

"There's too much fat—cream, egg yolks, bacon, sausage, ham, and so on—and she cooks a lot of French stuff."

"Now I know why it tasted so good."

"You men don't know how to eat. That's why you have heart attacks and pass on prematurely like my poor Preston Lee—and leave us unfortunate women to face our final years alone."

"My heart's fine as far as my doctor and I can tell."

"In your health, Edward, as in many other ways, you're the exception to the rule. Most men your age are fat, bent-over wrecks with no hair. You should see some of my high school classmates!"

* * *

44

A Coffin for Callahan

Sitting on his bench after Mrs. Davis went home, waiting for the bluebirds to show themselves, Callahan made a quick mental calculation of the weight of his coffin. If the lid and floor each weighed seventy-five pounds, and the sides weighed around forty pounds each, and the head and toe ends together weighed another twenty pounds, then the coffin weighed more than two hundred pounds. Throw in Callahan with a suit and shoes, a lining, and some handles, and the whole package was likely to weigh nearly four-fifty. With six pallbearers, each would have to shoulder seventy-five pounds. Most of Callahan's contemporaries couldn't lift anywhere near that much. If he had eight pallbearers, each of them would still have to carry more than fifty pounds, so if Callahan lived very long, he wouldn't have any friends strong enough to carry him. Maybe I should put wheels on it, he thought, and chuckled.

Next, he began to ponder the construction details. For a coffin to look finished and suitable for holding the departed, it should not show any nails or screws—or at least that's what the instructions said. There were two ways to accomplish this. First, one could screw directly through the bottom into the side pieces, taking care to countersink the holes so that a wooden plug could be glued in to hide the screw head. The second method would be to attach the frame rails to the sides from the inside, and then screw through these, also from the inside— first to the bottom piece and then to the side pieces. If the screws are not too long and put in correctly, they would never show on the exterior, leaving a perfectly smooth surface. Callahan preferred the second method. He thought screw holes filled with plugs looked precious (another word he would not have used—in relation to woodworking anyway), and besides, he didn't want to be bothered to make all the plugs and sand them smooth.

He carefully laid out each of the frame rails adjacent to the side piece to which it applied. He then drilled holes to connect the rails to the sides and another set at a right angle to the first to connect the rails to the bottom. The hardened steel screws—a dollar-fifty each—had been factory coated with a medium brown, corrosion-resistant finish to ensure that their heads would be nearly invisible in the purpleheart as it aged. (Not that anyone would be looking inside his coffin to check the screws, he assumed.)

To ensure a strong fit, wood glue would be used in addition to the screws wherever wood contacted wood. For so-called "natural" burials, coffin makers remove the screws after the glue has set so that there will be no metal in the coffin. Certain cemeteries insist on this. Callahan figured the funeral director could worry about it. Besides, if Callahan chose to be cremated, someone could sift his ashes to get the screws out if they liked, or just leave them in. He didn't think he would care at that point.

He began working at the head end, carefully gluing and clamping the frame rails all around the periphery of the coffin sides. A rail piece of appropriate length was glued to each of the six sides—top, bottom, long side left, long side right, short side left, and short side right. He then inserted and tightened each screw. He used a screw every six inches all the way around for a total of 32 screws. It was exacting and boring work, but he was pleased that everything seemed to fit snugly and he hadn't made any stupid mistakes.

When all the screws were in, he quit for the day. Although the label on the bottle claimed that the glue would set in four hours, he'd always favored giving glue plenty of time to work. He closed up the shop, planning to start attaching the side pieces first thing the next morning.

Twelfth

From Finley's Bar, the low-lying peninsula where Carter Wingate's house was situated, to the middle of Scarborough Sound, where the water was well over 50 feet deep, was about 8 nautical miles. The Whaler could make the round trip easily in a couple of hours. If the clouds stayed thick, it would be dark all the way. Without using navigation lights, Wingate headed his boat out into the creek. He knew the area well and had little doubt he could make the trip safely without lights if he held a moderate speed and kept a good lookout. Besides, he had a GPS that showed a chart and his own position in real time. In the faint green glow of the screen, he smiled. He looked at his reflection on the screen and smiled again.

His plan was simple. Take Hazel Jones's body out into the deep channel and throw it overboard, weighted to make sure it stays down. Rely on the summer heat and the abundant scavenging animals to reduce her to a skeleton in a few days. The skeleton will sink and be buried under the shifting sediment at the bottom of the channel. From personal experience, Wingate knew where the most popular fishing spots were, and he would be careful not to drop his victim close to any of them. He would also take care to navigate south of Watts Island and avoid Robin Hood Bar and California—no point in allowing an angler to spoil his plan by making a surprise catch.

After about ten minutes of cruising, when he was nearly past the flashing green light marking the entrance to St. George Creek, Wingate spotted a large motor yacht approaching him at high speed. This guy must be crazy, he thought, to come roaring into the creek at night with only daymarks and his GPS to guide him. It would be easy to miss the channel and run aground. Then he saw the yacht turn on a huge searchlight, presumably with the aim of finding the daymarks. It emitted a brilliant white beam at least a quarter mile long. At this point Wingate realized he was likely to be spotted, maybe even hailed and questioned about the best route into Port St. George. He didn't like this. If anyone saw him out in the creek in the dark with no lights, they would remember it.

Wingate then did something he didn't normally do. He panicked. He had to get out of the searchlight's path quickly. The only thing to do was dump the body immediately and run for home. He killed the engine and put the concrete block on the gunwale. Then he grabbed the body of Hazel Jones under the armpits and heaved her naked, stiffening corpse over the side. The concrete block rolled into the water after the body, and both disappeared. He started the engine and motored smoothly and quietly to a position well away from the channel as the beam of the searchlight swept across his wake. He never looked back. If he had, he would have noticed that the water wasn't deep enough to sink the body completely, and that Hazel Jones's head was above water.

Disappointed that he had not executed his plan correctly, but confident that he had not been observed, he headed toward home as the large yacht faded from view and he could no longer hear its engine. Later, as he approached his dock, he realized he simply could have gone well out of the channel—the same way he did when avoiding the searchlight—until the yacht passed, and then continued with his original plan. It hurt to admit that he had goofed by dumping the body so hastily. Making mistakes contradicted his view of himself as someone who always had the upper hand. This would not do, so he quickly put it out of his mind.

Thirteenth

Callahan started toward the house, but began wondering about the bluebirds. He knew this would happen. Once he started caring about them, he couldn't leave them alone. Then, as he approached the bluebird house, he thought, this is stupid. I checked on these birds earlier today. So many interruptions might actually upset them. I'd better leave them alone. As he was about to turn back toward the house, he noticed a magnificent white yacht tied up a couple of hundred yards down the creek. He recalled a conversation he'd had the previous fall with her captain, a local guy who had been hired by a wealthy retired industrialist to keep his yacht shipshape. The captain lived a few miles down the creek from Callahan's house, and stopped home twice a year on his trips between Rhode Island where the owner and his wife summered and Florida where they wintered. The captain and Callahan usually met at the bakery or the town wharf, and had enjoyed many a lively conversation about boats and boating.

The boat was an elegant older design. No matter how many times Callahan saw her, she never failed to grab his attention. He gazed down the creek at the grand vessel, and pondered how much money a man would need to own and operate such a thing. His own boat was a fourteen-foot fiberglass skiff with a fifteen horsepower outboard, and even that seemed to be nothing but one costly repair after another. He could hardly imagine the pile of money it would take to maintain a seventy-foot yacht. To get a better look, he walked cautiously to the end of his rickety dock. Maybe, he thought, when I finish the coffin, I'll replace the cracked and warped boards on this dock before somebody gets hurt.

Looking down to avoid putting his foot through one of the spots where the decking was missing, he couldn't avoid seeing the body of a naked woman stuck beneath his dock. She was floating face down, bloated, and very pale, with her hair, arms, and legs extended. Her ankles were bound by a yellow nylon rope, the free end of which floated near the surface of the water. At first Callahan absorbed the scene passively, as he might have done if watching a TV documentary about drowning. Then it hit him: this is a real woman, dead under my dock. He reached for his cell phone and realized he'd left it in the house to charge. As quickly as he could without falling through gaps in the dock, he scrambled to the shore and ran toward his house.

* * *

The sheriff's office investigator glanced at his tape recorder, as if to confirm it had enough battery to continue. "Now, Mr. Callahan, if you don't mind, give me a little bit of your history—when did you come here to live on the Shore, where did you come from, etcetera."

"I moved here in 1993 after I retired."

"Are you married?"

"Until about six months ago. My wife died of cancer last December twenty-ninth."

"I'm sorry to hear that. When you were working, what kind of work did you do?"

"I was a beat cop in Philadelphia for twenty years."

"You're one of us, then."

"Not anymore. I'm retired."

"Do you work here on the Shore?"

"Nope. I've been fixing up my house and woodworking and loafing."

"Did you know the woman you found in the creek?"

"Never seen her before this morning."

"Any idea how she got there?"

"I didn't put her there, if that's what you're asking, but I can easily imagine how she got there."

"And how is that?"

"That rope on her ankles suggests she was tied to something, like a dock, a boat, or an anchor of some kind, and somehow she came loose. After that, she must have drifted here on the tide, or maybe a passing boat snagged the rope and towed her."

"You'd make a good investigator."

"Maybe so, but fortunately for me, I'm retired."

"Thanks for your help." The investigator put his recorder and notebook in his jacket pocket and walked up the lawn toward the street. The other people in the large group of police officers, volunteer firemen, and newspaper people had already left, taking the woman's body with them. Callahan looked down the creek at the sparkling white yacht. Did the lady come from there? he wondered.

Turning back toward the land, he saw Mrs. Davis on her back porch. She had been enjoying a ringside seat for the whole business, and he figured her next move would be to come over and offer him some food as a way to advance her interrogation. He decided to go into the house and pull something out of his freezer so he could say he'd already started dinner and didn't need anything.

As it happened, this ruse was unnecessary. Mrs. Davis inexplicably stayed home and he microwaved his frozen dinner and ate it alone in blessed silence. Just as he was wondering whether to watch TV for a while or go to bed early, there was a gentle tapping on his door. "Yoo hoo, Edward," said Mrs. Davis, "are you home?"

"Yes, Eileen. I'm in the kitchen. Come on in."

She entered the room, looked at the frozen dinner wrapper, and screwed up her face as if she were about to comment on Callahan's eating habits, but instead asked, "Did you hear the latest?"

"Probably not," he replied dryly.

"That woman you found under your dock came from Taylors, South Carolina. Her name is Hazel Jones, and she has a daughter who lives in New York and a husband who's in prison."

"What for?"

"Murder." Mrs. Davis's face contorted in a look of pain. "Imagine being married to a murderer and then being murdered yourself."

"If he's in prison, at least he's one guy who's in the clear."

"The daughter's coming here in a few days to claim the body. That's what my nephew says. He's a deputy." Mrs. Davis could barely contain her delight that she had a personal contact inside the sheriff's office.

"If he's a deputy, he should be keeping quiet about what he knows. Perpetrators love to find out what the investigators know and what they don't. It helps them cover their tracks, or even intimidate or kill witnesses."

"His revelations are safe with me."

"But, Eileen, you've already told me."

"You're different. You're an investigator, too. He's hoping you can help the investigation."

"I already told the county people all I know."

"He means professional advice, from your days with a big city police force. People around here don't know anything about heinous crimes like what happened to Mrs. Jones. In big cities they have lots of experience. I told him to come over this evening. You don't mind, do you?"

Of course, Callahan *did* mind, but it was too late now. Mrs. Davis had helped him measure his shoulders, so he owed her one. Besides, at that moment a car with a young man at the wheel had just parked in Mrs. Davis's driveway—undoubtedly the nephew. He would scold him about blabbing case details all over town and send him away. That would be his professional advice: shut up and do your own investigating. There are no short-cuts.

"Yoo hoo—Willie!" Mrs. Davis shouted. "Come on in." The young man did as instructed and Callahan met him when he came onto the porch. Mrs. Davis introduced him as Deputy Willie Custis, Jr., who in her estimation was the most promising new member the Accomack County Sheriff's Office had had in years. Then she said she would go home and make some sweet tea.

Callahan went for a direct approach. "So, Willie, I hear you're working on the investigation of Hazel Jones's murder."

"Not exactly, Mr. Callahan. I'm very interested in it, of course, as everybody in the county is, but right now I'm assigned to traffic enforcement and patrol duty."

"How long have you been with the department?" Wearing a T-shirt, shorts, and sneakers that looked a size too big, Willie appeared to Callahan to be too young and fragile to be any good at police work. He couldn't imagine this kid being capable of dealing with some of the ruffians he'd had to handle in his time.

"Thirteen months next Friday. I graduated from the academy last May."

"Won't your homicide investigators be annoyed if you tread on their turf?"

"I don't mean to tell them, unless of course I discover something important they've missed. I'm just trying to enhance my investigative skills by following along, informally you could say."

"You're likely to damage your career doing that."

"Do you think so?"

"Affirmative. I'm kind of an expert on damaged police careers."

"Aunt Eileen says you were an expert investigator."

"She exaggerates. I spent most of my twenty years in traffic enforcement and routine patrol duty—just like you."

"Oh." The young deputy's face fell, and he stared at the floor.

"Here comes your aunt with our sweet tea."

Callahan turned the conversation, rather skillfully, he thought, to Willie—where he'd gone to high school and college, why he went into police work, and whether he had a girlfriend. Mrs. Davis kept trying to bring up the investigation, and Callahan kept changing the subject. In addition to Willie's personal history, they covered fishing, baseball, bluebirds, and the excellence of Mrs. Davis's cooking. The conversation ended when Willie mentioned that he had night duty that evening and had better get home and put on his uniform. As he left, Callahan thought, he's a good kid, and would make a decent officer if he only had a less romantic view of his job.

Fourteenth

Wingate slept well. His blunder in dumping the body too soon the night before became obscured by a cloud of self-satisfaction that developed as he enjoyed his morning coffee. He had eliminated the only person who cared about the events of his past, so blue skies and calm seas lay ahead. He couldn't be happier.

Orion, on the other hand, continued to sulk. After only playing with his breakfast, he began lurking next to the freezer. Maybe he wants his leash after all, thought Wingate. He removed the bundle of Hazel Jones's belongings from the freezer and let the Scottie examine the leash again. The reaction was the same. After a quick sniff, Orion fled to a corner. The dog can detect the smell of death, thought Wingate. I'll need to burn this stuff. This was not the result he had hoped for. He was reluctant to part with his victim's clothes and the leash because these items were tangible evidence of his severing a troublesome link with the past. He knew he would have enjoyed getting these objects out someday and handling them again. Reliving past triumphs was one of his particular pleasures, and disposing of Hazel Jones ranked near the top of his list of lifetime victories. But if Orion could detect something, probably a police investigation would also, especially since their technology had improved greatly in recent years. Wingate was not a man to take chances.

However, today was not a day for burning anything. He had some chores to do first. His boat had needed cleaning for a while, and in light of Wednesday night's activities, a thorough scrubbing was in order. He quickly assembled the necessary cleaning materials and implements, and soon was ready to head for the dock before the sun rose any higher and made the job unpleasant. He called Orion to join him. After some coaxing, the Scottie followed his master to the boat dock, but as soon as the cleaning process began, retreated to the house. Wingate rationalized this behavior by reminding himself that dogs hate the odor of bleach.

As he began cleaning, Wingate noticed that his neighbor had come home from wherever he had been the night before. He had never liked the kid. There were three strikes against him in Wingate's book. First, his parents were rich Chicago retailers, so he lived mostly off checks from home, whereas Wingate, at least in his own view, had earned every dollar he possessed by hard work and using his wits. He despised remittance men like his neighbor. Second, the boy was an environmentalist. He lived in a minuscule solar-powered home he built himself from recycled materials and smugly, relentlessly campaigned against plastics, particularly plastic bags and other merchandise containers. The kid thought they were wasteful and contributed to litter—one of several man-made blights affecting the Eastern Shore of Virginia. His campaigning annoyed Wingate because plastics, especially plastic food containers, was the business in which Wingate had started his career. The public wanted plastic for convenience and low cost. Wingate and his employers had supplied the product. As far as Wingate was concerned, that was the whole story. Screw the environment!

The third detestable feature of the young neighbor was that he was a neighbor at all. When Wingate bought his property, he had inquired about the lot next door and had been told it was not for sale, yet only a year later the kid showed up and occupied the place. This defeat was galling, and it made Wingate very angry every time he thought of it.

Fifteenth

Callahan did not sleep well. Images of Hazel Jones's lifeless body in the creek persisted in his mind even as he sipped his morning coffee. He went to look at the bluebirds, but even that produced little relief. At length, he realized that what he needed was companionship—somebody to talk to—but not Mrs. Davis, who would only offer words of wisdom while pumping him for information. He went to the bakery in search of another soul to share his thoughts, and his luck was good. Delbert Dix was sitting alone at a back table, fiddling with his electronic tablet.

"Good morning, Delbert. How are things?"

"Better for me than they probably are for you," he replied. "Did you really find a body on your dock yesterday?"

"Not on it; under it. In the creek. Under the water—not a pretty sight."

"Was she dead when you found her?"

"Definitely."

"Foul play?"

"That's everybody's assumption at the moment."

"So I've heard, but do you vote with the majority?"

"I suppose so, although it's not hard to imagine someone wanting to drown herself and using an anchor to make sure that if she changed her mind after jumping in, she couldn't turn back."

"That could be it."

"Maybe, but did she bring a length of rope and an anchor with her all the way from South Carolina? And why would she take off all her clothes first? And where are her clothes, anyway? Suicide doesn't seem likely to me."

As they spoke, Delbert was reading the online version of the local radio station's "Community News" on his tablet. "Says here they've made an arrest."

"Anybody I know?"

"It's filthy Pete."

"Never heard of him."

"Peter McDonald, an old sex offender. When I was in elementary school, he was convicted of indecency for taking pictures in the girls' locker room at the high school. He was a custodian there, and he set up a hidden camera that he could operate from his janitor's closet. He took pictures of local girls naked in the shower, printed them in his home darkroom, and hid them under his bed. His mom found them and turned him in. If I remember correctly, he got a year and half suspended. And naturally he was fired from his job as a school custodian."

"Okay, but what evidence connects Pete to Hazel Jones?"

"The paper says he fishes often in St. George Creek and was seen in his boat on the creek the same afternoon you found her body."

"But the witness didn't see him throw her in, right?"

"They believe she was sexually assaulted."

Callahan had picked up his coffee and cookie and was reading the online article over Delbert's shoulder. "It doesn't say anything about sexual assault in this article."

"I heard that part from my cousin. He's a deputy sheriff."

"Would that be Willie Custis, Jr.?" Callahan explained how he met Willie on Saturday, then added: "Our local sheriff's office leaks like a sieve."

"That's just small town culture. Everybody's used to telling everything they know to everybody else all the time."

"Somebody doesn't tell."

"Who?"

"The killer. Mrs. Jones was killed by a real person—someone who stripped off her clothes and tied something to her body to make it sink and stay down, then dumped it in the creek. That implies a local individual who doesn't share your small town desire to tell all."

"Maybe it's Pete, and he's being stubborn and refusing to confess."

"I hope he never confesses, because he more than likely didn't do anything. He's a keyhole peeper. Guys like that rarely have the guts to say 'Good morning' to a woman, much less kill one and dump her naked into a creek. Besides, the body had been in the creek for a while when I saw it, so if he was out fishing at around the same time, he's not the one."

"Did you know," asked Delbert, "that this is not the first time they've found a murdered woman's body in a creek around here?"

"You're kidding. When?"

"Nineteen fifty-six."

"Oh, you had me going for a minute. I thought you meant recently."

"Her name was Agnes Lodge, and she was thirty years old. A fisherman found the body, so he tied a rope around her ankle and towed the body to Bullbeggar Bridge where they held an initial inquest."

"Cause of death?"

"Hit on the head and shot with a rifle. She'd been missing since before Christmas and her body was only found in mid-February. She was wearing a nightgown."

"So, who did they arrest?"

"Nobody. Her husband disappeared about the same time she went missing and was never found."

"Sounds like he's the one. But Hazel Jones's husband is in jail down south, so they'll need to find somebody else after they figure out Pete's not their man."

At that moment, Callahan looked up and saw a young woman—too slender for her own good in his opinion—with dark, thoughtful eyes, a camera hanging from her neck, and the strap of a laptop case over her shoulder. "Are you Mr. Callahan?"

"Yes."

"I'm Melody Farley, from the *Eastern Shore News*. Got a minute?"

Callahan looked down at his coffee and cookie. He'd barely touched either one. He obviously had a minute. "Sure," he said.

Ms. Farley talked very quickly, as if she were in a hurry to catch a plane, or maybe needed the bathroom. "You found the victim's body yesterday, right?"

"Yes, but I wouldn't call her a victim. We don't know how she died."

"Everybody says she was murdered."

"The sheriff also?"

"Not yet, exactly. But they arrested somebody, so I just assumed, because everybody's saying that."

"Could be suicide."

"You really think so?"

"It's not very likely, but that's why investigators investigate, to find out."

"You were a police investigator, yourself, no?" offered Delbert, bringing up a subject Callahan had hoped would not become fodder for the press. Never tell anybody in a small town anything you want to keep to yourself was a lesson he had been slow to learn.

"I was a beat cop." Callahan replied, glancing from Delbert to Melody and back. "I started my career thinking I might do investigations, but later switched to traffic enforcement and various general duties."

Melody was on the scent now. "Didn't you like investigations?"

"They were fine, and can be interesting sometimes."

"So, if they were interesting, why did you change?"

"It's a long story." He stared into her dark eyes. "Maybe we should stick to the local investigation and leave the past in the past."

They discussed the body in the creek for a few more minutes, but when Melody determined there was little more to discover, she left quickly, leaving Callahan and Delbert to finish their coffee and sweets.

"Nice looking girl," said Delbert.

"Too skinny for me," Callahan replied. "If she were my daughter, I'd be trying to make her eat more, and maybe slow down some. She talks so fast, I can hardly follow what she's saying."

"Most young women these days are like that. Always rushing. No time for contemplation—or anything else for that matter."

A Coffin for Callahan

While he consumed his snack, Callahan read the rest of the online article. It stated that a woman's naked body had been found in the north branch of St. George Creek and that a retired policeman from Philadelphia named Edward Albert Callahan had discovered it. The sheriff's office had identified the victim as Hazel Jean Jones, a visitor from South Carolina, near Greenville. She was further described as the wife of Robert Lawrence Jones, who was currently in prison for committing a murder in 1981. The victim had been the bookkeeper at Dixiecraft Manufacturing, the company where he and Mrs. Jones both worked, and was the wife of a local Baptist minister. After her husband's prison term began, Mrs. Jones continued to work at Dixiecraft for several years until she retired to start a needlecraft shop, which she recently sold. The article concluded by saying Mrs. Jones is survived by one child, a daughter who works in New York City.

* * *

The rest of Callahan's day passed uneventfully. He went to the workshop and puttered, accomplishing little. He sat on his bench for a while and watched the bluebirds and other wildlife in his back yard. He couldn't focus on anything. Images of Hazel Jones's body in the water beneath his dock kept intruding. He felt as if he should have done something to save her. He wanted to turn the clock back and give her another chance at life. Why do I think such nonsense? he wondered.

Later than evening, Callahan was finishing putting away his dinner dishes when the phone rang. "Hello, Officer Callahan," said Willie Custis, Jr. "I thought I'd call to keep you up to date."

Callahan wasn't sure he wanted to be kept up to date, but it was too late now. "They let Pete McDonald go."

"When?"

"About an hour ago. His mother came in and gave him an alibi, and I told the sheriff what you told Delbert about peeping Toms. By the way, the official term we use now is "criminal voyeur." After I spoke to the sheriff, they let Pete go."

"But this isn't your investigation."

"That's true, but I believe they appreciated me passing along what you said."

Callahan tried to explain to Willie that most people didn't like others involving themselves in police matters as volunteers, however good their intentions, and even if they were sheriff's deputies. He also tried to explain the concept of departmental turf, and how the sheriff's office's investigators might resent Willie's offers of unsolicited information, and especially his telling tales of the investigation's progress to people all around the county. Callahan's arguments seemed to make no impression, so he wished Willie good night and headed upstairs to bed.

Sixteenth

Carter Wingate was making plans. As soon as he finished cleaning his boat, he would start preparing for a trip to Cape May, New Jersey. For months he had been negotiating by email with an elderly antique dealer there. The old man had in his shop an exceptional eighteenth century grandfather clock that Wingate coveted. He had a vision of this clock at head of his staircase, and had offered to trade three strings of pearls for the clock. He had been turned down flat because, in the dealer's estimation, it was not a fair trade. However, conditions had changed recently, and Wingate saw an opportunity. The dealer was now suffering from a recurrence of bladder cancer, which he had believed was cured many years ago. His medical bills were mounting, and he needed cash. Wingate had been hammering away with the idea that the pearls would be easier to sell than the clock, and that the original deal was a good one. It looked as if the old man was about to relent, so Wingate was preparing to strike.

The pearls he had never liked. He only bought them because he could do so at a fraction of their market value from a widow suffering from dementia. Since the pearls had been obtained at a bargain price, the net effect of trading what Wingate called "pearls from the old swine" for the clock would be to obtain the historic timekeeper for roughly a quarter of its assessed value. Wingate needed to act quickly, however, before the ailing dealer died or came to his senses and backed out.

Although Cape May was a fertile hunting ground for elderly suckers, Carter Wingate had never liked the place. To soften the blow of such a disagreeable visit, he would run up to Atlantic City as soon as he had secured the clock. There he could indulge his passion for beating the unwary at poker, and maybe even get lucky with a young member of one sex or the other.

The key to Wingate's winning at poker was his uncanny ability to read the psychology of his fellow players from small gestures and actions. It was as if he had a polygraph in his head. He could tell who was bluffing, who was confident, who was feeling lucky, and so on, merely from watching people. As for himself, he was so absorbed in watching others and matching his play to their apparent mental states that he tended to give off an air of inscrutable self-absorption. He could read them, but he was unreadable. To the casual player, he was a white-haired, very quiet Southern gentleman who liked to play cards, and to them he might have seemed an easy mark—somebody you could ignore even as the stakes got higher and higher because he seemed so friendly, bland, and unimportant. It also helped that most northerners seemed to believe that anyone with a strong Southern accent was stupid, and therefore didn't deserve close scrutiny. When he walked away from the table with all the chips he could fit in both hands and his pockets, the disappointed losers attributed his success to a run of spectacular luck, never detecting that he was actually a methodical harvester of other people's money.

Wingate's approach to poker reflected his approach to life. He believed in being prepared and having a solid plan, and based on these preferences he could be described as a cautious person. But, on the other hand, after having made appropriate preparations, he loved to take great risks, like betting several thousand dollars on a poker hand. He hated losing, of course, but he rarely lost, and when he did, he used it as a learning opportunity.

For Wingate, sex was another game, different in nature but not in essence from beating his tablemates at poker or fleecing the innocent of their antique possessions. There was pleasure to be obtained in the physical experience, of course, but the special excitement for Wingate was the hunt—selecting his quarry, using his considerable skills to charm and persuade, and if these fail, using the contents of his locket ring to compel the reluctant to yield. The point was that he wanted access to other peoples' bodies and he got it. One would never call what he did making love. It was a form of theft, and humiliation of the victim made it all the sweeter.

Seventeenth

On Saturday morning Callahan decided it was time to try to push Hazel Jones out of his head—which was not easy, because he had dreamt about her much of the night—and accomplish something useful. As a start, he would check on the bluebirds. After completing that mission and on his return to his house, he saw Mrs. Davis walking quickly toward him across the lawn. "They've got the right one this time," she declared. Callahan did not have to ask who they'd got, because she volunteered this information before he could frame the question. "That Bullfrog has always been a bad one, as anyone might expect, because rotten apples never fall far from the tree. Anyone who'd known his daddy could have told you he'd be the one to do something like this."

The story, as related by Mrs. Davis, was that a man named Haywood Smith, also known as Bullfrog because he was a huge man who liked to swim in creeks and ponds spearing fish, had been brought in for questioning regarding the Hazel Jones murder. That Smith might be the perpetrator seemed obvious to Mrs. Davis for two reasons—he'd been in trouble with the law frequently over a period of many years and his father had killed a man in the nineteen-fifties in a dispute related to a car accident. The probable third reason, which she didn't mention, was that Haywood Smith was black or, as she would have said, "colored." She also neglected to mention that the killing by the senior Smith had been ruled justifiable homicide because the man he killed had been beating him on the head with a pipe at the time Smith stabbed him.

A Coffin for Callahan

To Callahan, the arrest of Bullfrog didn't seem any more likely to lead anywhere than the arrest of filthy Pete, but he did not argue. He had always believed that people who had nicknames or aliases were likely to be guilty of something, since they clearly wanted to have more than one self. However, the chance that a local black man with a police record would suddenly be inspired to kill a white female tourist seemed remote. There could be some connection, of course, but Bullfrog didn't quite ring true as a suspect. Callahan listened patiently to Mrs. Davis and then excused himself to go shopping for something for dinner. He had plenty of food in his freezer, but going shopping was the only excuse he could invent at that moment.

* * *

At the supermarket he ran into Delbert Dix, who had also heard the news about Bullfrog. "He seems a more likely suspect than filthy Pete," he offered.

"My neighbor told me a little about it," said Callahan, unloading his two items onto the conveyer belt. "Had this guy ever been involved with this kind of violence before?"

"No, but he's been in lots of trouble—selling drugs, making moonshine, and punching people at parties—stuff like that."

"Were any of his victims white?"

"Not that I ever heard. He pretty much stuck to his own community, which is basically poor black folks."

"I wonder why the sheriff's office believes such a man would suddenly get it into his head to assault a white female visitor from out of state, whom he doesn't know, strip her, strangle her, and then try to hide his crime by sinking her in the creek."

"They must have their reasons." Delbert looked thoughtful, and then a bit anxious. "Hey, how come you know she was strangled?"

"I don't, but the paper said she didn't drown, and when I found her there was nothing indicating she had been shot, stabbed, or beaten to death. She was definitely dead before she went in the water, so that's about all that's left, except maybe poison. And," he added with a smile, "if they'd found poison in her system, I'm sure Willie would have told me."

Upon returning home, and after sorting his mail and throwing away most of it, Callahan made a peanut butter and jelly sandwich—his usual lunch, which he washed down with iced tea and dutifully followed with an apple, a once-a-day finisher Doris had always insisted on so he would have a balanced diet and good digestion. He was pondering how best to spend the afternoon, and thinking he might finally try to launch his boat. It was well past the time of year when most people put their boats in the water, and he had been procrastinating. This afternoon would be perfect for boat launching, he thought, but he hadn't even begun before he was interrupted.

"Edward?" inquired Mrs. Davis, rapping gently on his screen door. "I have something for you."

He went to the front door, and saw Mrs. Davis holding a plastic food container. By her side stood Willie Custis, Jr., looking very smart, but still rather young and skinny, in his immaculate new uniform.

"Hello Eileen, . . .Willie."

A Coffin for Callahan

"I made some coleslaw for you," said Mrs. Davis with a flash of a smile. "As usual, I got carried away and made too much. You know what they say, 'Waste not, want not,' so I decided you should have some."

"Thanks. You're very kind," he replied. Callahan hated this. He could feed himself, but he couldn't think of a polite way to stop Mrs. Davis from "helping" him. "Maybe Willie needs some," he said, knowing as he spoke that resistance was futile.

"I've already set aside a container for him, too, and since we're both here, I thought now was a good time for him to ask you about the investigation."

So that was what the coleslaw was for, Callahan thought, a bribe so Willie could get some free advice. "Why don't we all sit on the porch," he said. He wasn't about to concede any more ground by letting Mrs. Davis and Willie into his house. "What do you want to know?"

"Well, Mr. Callahan," he said, "I guess I just wanted your opinion about whether you think Bullfrog Smith is the man we're after."

"I'm not sure how I would know that," Callahan replied. "After all, I don't have the evidence your office has collected. I only know what your aunt has told me."

"To be honest, we don't know a lot more."

"If that's all you have, you're not likely to get a conviction, because you can't tie him to the crime without some physical evidence or an eyewitness. It won't matter whether he's the perpetrator or not, he'll walk."

"That's what I thought you might say, and I told one of the investigators the same thing this morning."

"You told him I would say that?"

"It just sort of slipped out that I'd been talking to you, and he said 'So what does the big city cop Callahan think?' and I said I didn't know, but I thought you would say there wasn't enough evidence. He said he would find more evidence."

"Willie," said Callahan, not knowing whether he was a good enough actor to scold properly without laughing, "You've got to learn to keep your mouth shut. Listening is a virtue. Speaking out of turn can land a man in a lot of trouble."

"I'm not sure what you mean."

"A good investigator gathers his facts and keeps them to himself until he has a case. Even then, he only shares them with the prosecutor and other members of his team. Scattering information and opinions all over town is a good way to blow your case, or end your career, or maybe both at the same time."

"Loose lips sink ships," said Mrs. Davis.

"I'll try to do as you say, Mr. Callahan, but if I get something good, do you want me to let you know?"

"No, I do not. If you must tell somebody, share your information with your investigators, not with civilians like me."

After Mrs. Davis and Willie left, Callahan was finally ready to go prepare his boat for launching when his phone rang.

"Mr. Edward Callahan?"

"That's me," he replied, surprised to get a call from a person who sounded like a young woman. Another reporter?

"This is Felicia Jones. I'm going to be in Accomack County soon to get my mom's car and her remains. May I visit you for a few minutes so I can thank you in person for finding her and for your help in the investigation of her death?"

He couldn't say no, even though he wasn't at all eager to have such an encounter, which he was certain would be very emotional. But he wondered how Ms. Jones got the idea he was investigating. She explained that she was arriving Monday afternoon and wondered if she could visit him then.

"No problem, but the closest bus stop is at a gas station in Exmore, about fourteen miles from here. How are you going to get to Port St. George? Should I meet you?"

"Thanks, but that's taken care of. The sheriff assigned one of his deputies and I've already spoken to him. He sounds very nice. His name is Willie Custis, Jr. He said he would meet me and take me to where they've been keeping my mother's car. He also said he could show me the way to your house."

"He definitely knows how to get here," Callahan replied. He couldn't resist a smile. Living in a small town, you can't get away from anything.

Eighteenth

Wingate finished cleaning his boat and returned to the house for lunch. Orion was asleep in his corner, and only opened one eye, scratched his ear, and looked up wanly as his master approached. "Come on, buddy, stop being such a hang-dog," said Wingate, as he went to collect the mail from the box on the porch. Saturday's mail had little of interest. He had few friends or relatives—none of them close—and nearly all of his business arrangements were made by email.

Among the usual pizza shop flyers and letters urging him to sign up for cable or satellite TV, the only items of interest to Wingate were the two local papers—the free one and the subscription one—both of which he had delivered. He did not like most of the articles, which seemed far too hometown and ho-key for his taste, but he always wanted to be up to date on developments in local government that might cost him money. He also liked to check out the auction notices and bankruptcy sale announcements. He was not a man to miss an opportunity.

Anticipating his trip to Cape May, he almost set the papers aside, but a difference in the free paper caught his eye. Instead of its usual fold, it was wrapped in yellow paper with "MUR-DER!" printed on it in red letters. Sensing he would find bad news, he tore off the wrapper and saw a one-page flyer with the headline "Shocking Discovery in Port St. George: Naked Woman Found in Creek."

The story described how a woman had been discovered Friday morning in St. George Creek, after the regular paper had been printed. Not wanting to miss a scoop, the paper had printed an extra edition on a sheet of copy paper. According to the article, the Accomack County Sheriff's Office, an organization for which Wingate had scant regard, had tentatively identified the woman, but was withholding the name until next of kin could be notified. Wingate's first reaction was that it was amazing that there would have been two murders of women who were dumped naked into St. George Creek in one week, and if so, what good luck that was for him, because if Hazel Jones were ever found, they would assume that the same perpetrator had done both.

Next, he experienced a moment of panic, because a far more likely explanation was that his cinder block anchoring system had failed somehow and the body of Hazel Jones had drifted nearly four miles into town. His heart rate returned to normal when he realized that it could have been much worse. The body was discovered far from where he dumped it, and was miles from his house. It had become stuck under someone's dock not more than three hundred yards from Duck's Store Restaurant, so if the connection were to be made with Hazel Jones's visit there, it would be assumed that she was murdered near the restaurant (true) and dumped there (false). Actually, having her found near the restaurant was probably the best alternative if she had to be found at all. He relaxed and read the rest of the article, which said that the sheriff's office investigator had some suspects in mind already. And none of them are me, thought Wingate with satisfaction as he went upstairs to start packing for his trip.

Nineteenth

An hour or so after lunch, Callahan finally made it to the corner of his back yard where his boat had been parked all winter. He pulled off the tarp and found everything to be more or less in order: no squirrel nests, only a few cobwebs and wasp nests, and no leaves blown under the tarp to make a mess. This year he didn't even need to re-inflate the tires on the trailer. He poured some fresh gas mix into the outboard and tried a quick start. It roared after only three pulls, and he immediately shut it off.

After a bit of backing and filling, he had the trailer hooked to his pickup, and at that point he even remembered to put the drain plug back into the boat. After driving a few feet and stopping to check that the trailer wheels were not frozen from rusted bearings, he continued to the town wharf. Nobody was blocking the ramp, and he launched with ease. He parked the truck, hopped into the boat, and was soon cruising up the north branch of the St. George Creek toward his house. It was a treat to be back on the water. He wasn't much of a boater, and he rarely fished, but he found riding on the creek in his little boat to be immensely pleasurable. He loved the feel of the water beneath him and the unique view of the world afforded when afloat.

He tied up at his dock and started walking back to the town wharf to retrieve his truck. When he was about halfway there, his cell phone rang.

"Mr. Callahan?"

"Yes."

"It's Willie."

"What can I do for you, Willie?"

"I know you told me not to tell you things, but I thought you ought to know. The sheriff had to let Bullfrog Smith go."

"Why?"

"They found out he was in jail overnight in Delaware when the murder of Mrs. Jones happened. The Seaford Police Department didn't let him out of jail until long after the medical examiner says she died. He couldn't possibly be the right one."

"Lucky for him."

"For Bullfrog, maybe, but the sheriff's really mad now. The investigators thought he was a perfect suspect, and they lost him, so the pressure is on to find somebody else."

"Thanks, Willie." Callahan continued his walk. It often goes like this, he thought. Investigations are frequently driven by politics. It's critical to a department's public relations to keep the citizenry from finding out that its investigators don't have a clue. You grab anybody who's handy and try to build a case around who you've got rather than persisting until you find the real perpetrator. It looked as if the sheriff's office was falling into that trap. He wondered who the next unlikely suspect would be.

Driving home, he started worrying about the condition of his house. Doris had always been rather house-proud. It was one of those things that went along with being raised in a working class section of Philadelphia. Callahan always helped her clean if she asked him to, which happened rarely (because, he suspected, he didn't do as good a job as she did). He had tried to keep house properly after she died, but knew he wasn't achieving her standard of neatness. However, the imminent arrival of Ms. Jones started him worrying. He didn't want the house to look poorly cared for. It would be an insult to Doris. He resolved that before Monday he would do a thorough vacuuming, mop the kitchen floor, and maybe even dust some things.

* * *

Callahan awoke Sunday morning feeling surprisingly well. He had slept soundly, perhaps because his recent progress on his coffin had been excellent and his boat was now in the water. The sun was shining. He even saw a bluebird on a hackberry branch outside his bedroom window. For the first time since Doris's death, he felt healed. But the good feeling troubled him. It seemed wrong that someone he had loved so much could be shed so easily. He didn't expect to mourn forever, but he felt the release from pain had come too soon. He wouldn't have minded suffering a few months longer. It would have seemed more respectful to her. But he felt great. He couldn't help it.

He hurried through breakfast and headed for the workshop. Attaching the coffin's side panels required a good deal more skill than merely attaching the frame rails. Two challenges had to be met. First, the bottom of the coffin didn't have any square corners. The angled edges meant that clamps would slip and then loosen unpredictably, making holding the pieces in place while inserting screws difficult. He overcame that obstacle by using the scraps from the original cuts to provide triangular shims that exactly fit the sides. (Like many woodworkers of his generation, Callahan never threw anything away, so naturally these scraps were still in the shop.) With a little double-sided tape on each scrap, they stayed in place, giving the clamps a square grip that held beautifully.

The second challenge was to make sure the bottom edges of each side stayed edge-matched to the bottom itself. This was accomplished by clamping some other scraps of the correct length to the inside surface of each side. If the top of the scrap lined up with the top of the side it was attached to, and stayed that way after a gentle tap with a wooden mallet, everything was in alignment, and the screws could be inserted and turned home.

Working methodically and with growing excitement as each side was attached, he continued from left foot to bottom to right foot to right shoulder. Then he took a stretch break for some coffee and a quick look at the bluebird house. Only the male was observed, and he seemed to be rushing from grass to house to marsh to house in a frenzy of activity. The female must be sitting on her eggs, Callahan thought, and he's bringing her food. Hatching of the second brood must be right around the corner. Bursting with positive feelings, he returned to his shop.

He finished the head end of the coffin and the left shoulder. He was done. The coffin looked splendid. He was delighted with his work and his own performance. To celebrate, he had an early lunch and then took his boat on a long, aimless cruise down the creek and back. It was a great day.

* * *

Callahan started the day Monday by going to his shop to work on his coffin, planning to continue the good run he had

had Sunday. Then he remembered the cleaning. He quickly put his tools away, cut off the electric power, and hurried into the house. In his excitement from doing so well with the coffin's side panels the day before, he had completely forgotten that he wanted make the house spic and span before Felicia Jones arrived. Even though Doris was no longer there, he knew that wherever she was she would be mortified if he ever let a visitor enter the house when it was not looking its best. It would be all the worse that the young visitor was grieving. Callahan could easily imagine how Doris would feel. A messy house will add to the young woman's grief, she would say. Their home needed to comfort the bereaved, and to do that it must be spotlessly clean, or at least that's how Doris would have put it.

He started at the top floor and vacuumed every room, both the floors and any horizontal surfaces that looked as if they might collect dust. He was shocked at how much dust he found. The house was a veritable resort hotel for dust bunnies—and he had thought he was doing a pretty good job— hadn't Mrs. Davis always told him so? Maybe she was merely being kind. Women have a funny way of doing that—telling little white lies to make men feel better, as if they didn't know that sooner or later the suckered males always discover the truth and feel worse than before.

After the vacuuming was done, he opened several windows for airing while he cleaned the kitchen counters, stove top, and behind the toaster and microwave, and then he mopped the kitchen and bathroom floors. He thought of cleaning some windows, but realized he would never get them all done before afternoon, and having some of them clean would only draw attention to the ones that weren't. He cleaned all the sinks and poured blue gunk in the toilet bowls, scrubbed them out, and flushed them clean. He started to spray air freshener around the house, but realized he'd never cared for the scent—Tropical Temptation, a ripe mango and lime combination—that Doris had loved, but he felt smelled like it would attract fruit flies. Instead, he would leave the windows open a while longer. He enjoyed the local fresh air with its marshy, muddy smell. May as well introduce the young lady to the Eastern Shore as it really is, he thought.

Twentieth

Wingate always enjoyed driving north from Virginia's Eastern Shore. He especially enjoyed it when he turned onto U.S. 113, a shadow to the main road that traversed a little of Maryland and half of Delaware, blending into a toll road near Dover Air Force base. This quiet byway reminded him of one of the things he had liked about the west, especially Nevada—roads with very little traffic. Deserted roads appealed to Carter Wingate because little traffic meant few people. Wingate didn't actually like human beings much, himself excepted, of course. He saw himself in a slightly Olympian way—distant—which is to say, superior to—his fellow members of the human race. He was confident of his superiority over the plebes he fleeced and the people like them who had nothing worth taking. His experience in life proved him right. People were beneath him, and they served only as prey or as objects for his sexual pleasure. When he wasn't in a predatory or lustful mood, the fewer humans around, the better. Route 113 was not as deserted as Nevada roads, but it was hardly ever busy, and he liked that.

At Millsboro, he stopped and bought a grilled chicken wrap, which he consumed on his way to the ferry terminal. He hated eating in the car because it was so messy and was something lower class people did, but he had to reach the ferry before quarter to eight or he'd miss the last crossing. Eating fast food and dripping some of it on his pants disgusted him, but it served its nutritional purpose and he was in line for the ferry well before the scheduled departure time.

Although he preferred being alone, once the ferry crossing began, Wingate found the car stifling with the air conditioning off, so he went up to the sun deck. The weather was fine and the crossing smooth, with a light southwesterly breeze stirring the humid air. He experienced a warm feeling of well-being as he watched the sun slowly sink over Delaware Bay. He had entirely forgotten tying the body of Hazel Jones to a concrete block and dropping it into St. George Creek. Instead his thoughts turned to the triumph anticipated for the next day, when he would finally get his grandfather clock in trade for a few unwanted pearls.

Wingate was thinking of walking around the periphery of the deck for the exercise when he happened to glance to his left and see a woman leaning against the rail, as he was, enjoying the sunset. Her dark hair extended nearly to her waist, and her tight black jeans and high heels seemed to say to him, "This is what you've been waiting for." Savoring the feeling that his trip might be more successful than he expected, he walked confidently to near where she stood.

"Beautiful evening," he said, leaning against the rail and moving closer.

"Isn't it, though?" She turned to face him, revealing a blouse unbuttoned enough to show her more than ample bosom.

"Headed for Cape May?" Wingate asked. He could feel a stirring in his trousers.

"Princeton. We're going to a conference on economics."

"We?" He smiled. "I don't see anyone else." He grinned and mimed looking around.

"My brother. He's down below, buying us drinks."

"Oh," said Wingate.

Twenty-first

His cleaning done, Callahan checked on the bluebirds, and then walked around his property looking for fallen branches to pick up and other garden bits that he could straighten up. Contemplating Ms. Jones's visit was making him antsy. With everything in and around the house as clean as he could make it, Callahan headed to the bakery for a coffee and a cookie. As he walked the three blocks, he realized that he'd been going to the bakery more than he used to. All the coffee and sweet treats couldn't possibly be doing him any good, but it was terrific comfort food, and he still felt the need for comfort, although, if someone had asked him, he wouldn't have said so. While standing in line, he met Delbert Dix, who also seemed to be coming to the bakery more often than before. Delbert was making good progress on his book, and offered Callahan another story of murder and mayhem on the Eastern Shore.

"There was this bootlegger named Ormond Nester, who frequently drove from Pocomoke, Maryland to the Eastern Shore of Virginia to sell liquor to distributors in the black community who then sold it to their neighbors and friends. Late one Friday night in 1925, he was discovered near Perkins City in his car, shot in the head. When the officers and the Commonwealth's Attorney—who did investigations himself in those days—searched the car, they found thirty-two half-gallon jars filled with corn whiskey.

"The initial suspect was a woman named Myrtle Perry of Wilmington, Delaware. She told the police she had been traveling with some other people on their way to Port St. George when they came upon the car with the dead Mr. Nester in it.

She claimed the others in her party panicked and drove away, leaving her alone with the corpse. To get away, she walked across farm fields trying to reach Perkins City, and finally received a ride from a passerby. When she went before the judge, however, her story became muddled, so they held her for questioning. Eventually she admitted that she had been with Nester, but she claimed a black guy—what they called 'colored' in those days—jumped on the running board of the car and shot Nester."

"Sounds like the black man was a figment of Myrtle's imagination."

"The authorities considered that. Based on the way Nester was shot—in the forehead, with the exit wound at the back of his skull, they couldn't see how Mrs. Perry avoided being shot at the same time."

"Did they get a conviction?"

"Yes, but not Mrs. Perry. Right after Nester's corpse was discovered, they also arrested five local black men as material witnesses, but then let two of them go. Then, about a month after the killing, the court cited what it called 'new developments' in the case and released Mrs. Perry. Three of the black men continued to be held in jail without bail."

"So they pinned it on the black men?"

"Not all of them. Two of the three were tried, and one was convicted. He got eighteen years."

"Maybe Mr. Nester wasn't playing straight with one of his distributors. That sort of thing explains many murders in the drug world even today."

A Coffin for Callahan

Upon returning home, Callahan began to wonder whether he should eat lunch or wait to offer lunch to Felicia Jones, although he hoped not, since PB&J seemed too informal. He called the gas station in Exmore where the bus stopped and learned it would be after 1:00 o'clock before the southbound coach arrived. Allowing for the time it would take for Willie to drive back to Port St. George, he had plenty of time. He made his usual sandwich and ate it while reading yesterday's paper.

Despite a cheery article about the upcoming Chincoteague pony penning, he couldn't stop thinking about the Hazel Jones murder, which had already lost the interest of the press. Not only did the crime lack a believable perpetrator, but it seemed pointless. Most of the murders he knew of, and all of those that Delbert had been sharing, had a clear back story—drugs, illegal alcohol, money, jealousy, pride—that set the stage for the deed. Hazel Jones's death seemed to have occurred for no reason. Of course, there was always the all-purpose reason of uncontrollable lust, prime motivator of a long line of serial killers and other weirdos who couldn't handle rejection. But there had been no previous such killings on the Shore—ever—or at least if there had been, Delbert had not mentioned them yet. Could this be the first in a series of serial murders of women? The thought was not comforting. Callahan headed to his workshop, determined to forget about murders and make some progress on his coffin.

He failed. He couldn't concentrate on the work at hand. To try and stay productive, he brushed the dust out of his table saw, replaced the blade, and sharpened his set of six wood chisels. None of these chores really needed to be done, but they were simple and kept his mind clear for thinking. However, all he could manage was to spin his mental wheels. He was getting nowhere and he was disappointed with himself. In his early days in Philadelphia, he had shown an aptitude for investigative work, and he assumed that these native skills would always be there, even if he'd rarely had a chance to use them during his two decades on the force. He could not make himself think productively, which disappointed him.

Frustrated by his lack of progress on either his coffin or the murder questions, and anticipating Felicia Jones's imminent arrival, his mind turned to replaying another one of Delbert's stories he'd heard in the morning—an example of an investigation that succeeded where his was faltering. Starting with the poetic headline "Death rode a U.S. mail sack into Cape Charles, Va.," the July 1936 newspaper story described how a well-liked local farmer named Stephen Poulson was killed by a bomb in a package he and his wife thought was a wedding gift. According to the news account, the explosion was heard a mile away. The blast partially blinded Poulson's young wife, and wrecked their car. Nothing was left of him but his head. Amazingly, Mrs. Poulson remembered seeing a spring pop up as the box was opened and briefly glimpsed a pipe-like object in the box. Thinking it was a practical joke, she was leaning away and opening the car door when the bomb exploded, saving her life.

The only clue available was a fragment of the package wrapping, which read F.C. Poulson, Richmond, Va." Despite this clue, nothing much happened in the investigation until early October. For ten weeks, the Postal Inspector's office and other investigators worked the case. Finally, they arrested a North Carolina dentist, who had employed Mrs. Poulson as an office assistant before she moved north and married.

A Coffin for Callahan

The investigators had discovered that Dr. L.M. Freedland, in addition to his dental skills, was a competent chemist and veteran of the First World War, where he may have gained experience with explosives. Shortly after his arrest and jailing in Eastville, Virginia, he slashed his wrist with a broken watch crystal. A few days later he broke his eyeglasses and tried again. This time he succeeded, because the prisoner assigned to keep an eye on him fell asleep. Three years later, the U.S. Senate voted to give a reward to two Virginia State Police officers and the mail clerk who helped investigators trace the package.

Callahan was impressed by how neatly all the loose ends had been tied together, an unusual outcome on the Eastern Shore or anywhere. He wondered if the killing of Hazel Jones would ever by resolved so well. He also spotted a part of the story he could use—a prior connection. Like the dentist, whoever killed Hazel Jones may have been motivated, not by the circumstances at the time of the killing, but by something from the past.

Twenty-second

A pudgy, gray-haired man with a long, scraggly beard walked toward them holding a pair of large plastic cups. "They only had Sprite. Sorry."

"That's okay," the woman replied. She took one of the large cups and sipped through its oversize straw. Wingate enjoyed watching her red lips close around the shiny plastic tube.

"Who's your friend?" asked the bearded brother.

The woman giggled. "I don't know." She turned to Wingate and extended her hand, "I'm June, who are you?"

"Carter," he replied.

"Carter, meet my brother, Alex."

The men shook hands. "So what brings you out on a beautiful evening like this, Carter?"

"I'm heading to Cape May to buy an antique clock." This was not the conversation Wingate wanted to have, but he couldn't think of a way to avoid it, and there was always the possibility that Alex would get lost somewhere or—he chuckled to himself—stumble over his own plump feet and fall overboard.

"For pleasure or for investment?"

"I would say a little of each. I've always wanted a clock like the one I'm buying, for aesthetic reasons, because it will go so well with some of the other things in my house, but naturally it will have some investment value as well I suppose." Instinctively, Wingate avoided any suggestion that he cared about money. It was a habit he had been practicing for years.

"Beware of baubles, Carter." Alex's face wrinkled in a concerned way.

"I'm not sure I understand." Making conversation with this guy while glancing at his sister's curvaceous body was making Wingate so angry he wanted to spit, but he did not betray himself and continued to smile warmly.

"Love of baubles is the first sign that you may be suffering from what I call addictive acquisitiveness or, as most people would say, uncontrollable greed."

"I feel fairly safe from that." He was becoming very angry now. This man Alex clearly had an agenda. Of course Wingate had his own agenda regarding June, and until he could get Alex out of the way it was going nowhere.

"It's like this." Clearly, Alex had warmed up to his favorite topic, and there was no stopping him now. "Have you ever noticed how people automatically dislike the overweight or the addicted? They puritanically judge such people, assuming they suffer from weakness of character. (Wingate conceded to himself that that was precisely what he thought when he was introduced to Alex.) The only people who avoid this condemnation are those who are obsessed with acquiring wealth. We demonize the fat, but lionize the rich. We deplore the chain smoker, but adore the chain acquirer."

To Wingate this felt like an attack. Despite knowing that, with people like Alex, any protest only eggs them on, he couldn't help himself and said, "But aren't people who try to better themselves the engine that drives our economy?"

"That's Republican Party, dark brown hooey to excuse their adoration of the rich capitalists who support their campaigns. When someone makes so much money he doesn't know what to do with it, and buys a twenty room house for a single person or a two hundred foot yacht when he doesn't even like boats, we don't say, 'This person is an idiot who wastes his life away making money, which he then spends on luxuries to justify his greed. He should see a psychiatrist or go to avarice rehab.' No way! Instead we say, 'Look at all the lovely things Mr. Goldsacks has bought. Let's do a magazine article or a TV special on his acquisitions so we can all pretend we're him and drool.' There's a lot more I can tell you about this, Carter, but I need to visit the men's room. I'll be right back."

"Your brother is very enthusiastic."

"He's obsessed."

"I've noticed." He smiled. "And you, June, are you obsessed?"

"As long as my paychecks keep coming, I don't worry much about that stuff."

"Then why don't you skip the economics conference and meet your brother on his way back. You and I could tour the lovely Victorian town of Cape May together tomorrow, and really enjoy each other's company. Then we could go up to Atlantic City where I plan to spend a day and a night at the casinos, and could have an even better time."

"Thank you for the kind offer, Carter, but my brother has narcolepsy, so I have to drive for him. I'm so sorry."

Twenty-third

Still pondering links with the past as he wiped off the kitchen counter for the second or third time, Callahan saw a sheriff's office car pull up to the curb outside his house. Deputy Willie Custis, Jr., looking surprisingly official in his perfectly pressed brown and tan uniform, emerged and gestured for a blue compact car with South Carolina tags to pull into Callahan's drive. When the car stopped in the drive, Willie gallantly opened the door for a young woman. As she walked in front of the deputy toward his house, Callahan was struck by how much she resembled her late mother—the same angular shoulders, the same strong jaw, and the same straw blonde hair. With a mixture of anticipation and dread, he opened the screen door and stepped out onto the porch.

"Hello, Mr. Callahan," she said. "It's very thoughtful of you to see me."

"It's no trouble at all. Please come in."

The three of them entered his living room and sat down. Up to now Callahan had not been particularly pleased to see Willie, but today he was glad the younger man was there. At a loss for words, he hoped Willie would provide some relief. Instead, Ms. Jones opened the conversation with one of his least favorite topics.

"Deputy Custis tells me you know nearly everything worth knowing about police work."

"He's exaggerating. I had twenty years on the force in Philadelphia, so I've seen a lot of things, but I certainly don't know everything."

"He says you've been right about the suspects in my Mom's death when the investigators were wrong."

"Maybe I'm a lucky guesser. How was your trip?"

"The trip sucked. I hope I never have to take another bus ride as long as I live."

"Would you like some tea, coffee . . . ?"

"Not right now, but thanks."

Willie stood up. "I'd better be going. I'm still on duty."

Felicia Jones rose and shook his hand. "Thank you so much for picking me up. It made getting to Port St. George so much easier."

Willie left quickly, and an awkward silence began. Callahan didn't know what to say, and for a moment it appeared his young guest didn't either. She started to cry. "I'm sorry," she said, taking a tissue out of her purse. "I thought I was doing better, but being in Mom's car again and meeting you and coming so close to where she died . . . I'm having trouble . . . .."

"It's only natural for you to be upset."

"Would you mind showing me where you found her?"

"Are you sure you want to see?" As he asked the question he knew her answer. Despite her tears, Felicia Jones had a look of determination on her face that impressed him.

"Yes. It'll be my only opportunity. I believe it's important for me to see where my mom died."

Not wanting to start a discussion about the exact location of death, Callahan led her out the back door. He would wait until later to explain that her mother did not die under his dock, and indeed nobody but Hazel Jones's murderer knew exactly where she died, which was a big part of the reason the investigation seemed to be going nowhere. On the way to the dock he showed Felicia the bluebird house and explained about the second brood. He was pleased that this seemed to distract her and that she was enthusiastic about the bluebirds and their family.

They walked out onto the dock, with Callahan taking care to point out where the bad boards were, as he silently scolded himself for not having taken the time to replace them before Felicia arrived. Again there was a period of silence. It was clear that she was waiting for him to say something. He didn't want to, but he knew his duty. "When I first saw her, she was floating a little below the surface, underneath the dock between these two posts here," he gestured, "and the end of the dock. She had a yellow nylon rope tied around her ankles."

"So she couldn't swim?"

"The investigators said she was not alive when she went in the water."

"How do they know?"

"No water in her lungs. She didn't drown."

"Oh." She put a hand out and rested it on one of the dock posts.

"Would you like go back to the house."

"No. Please tell me the rest."

Callahan cleared his throat. "They believe the rope was used to tie her body to a weight in an attempt to make it sink. Later on, one of our local watermen recovered a concrete block with the same kind of rope on it a few miles down the creek. Somehow the rope broke or got cut, maybe by a boat propeller, and she drifted here on the tide."

"How did she die?"

"She appears to have been strangled."

"Why?"

"Why do I say that or why did the perpetrator choose strangulation?"

"Both."

"Strangulation is what's left over after you rule out other causes, as the sheriff's office appears to have done. It could have been poison, but there was never any mention of that in the press or from our friend Willie, who can't keep his mouth shut."

"He's nice."

"True enough, but he needs to learn to keep department business to himself." Callahan was relieved that talking to Felicia Jones was not bothering him as much as he feared it would. She was a strong young woman. He felt proud of her. "As to why the murderer chose strangulation, I would say it was probably the only method available. He may not have had a weapon of any kind close by, so he used his hands."

"He?"

"Most likely. I wouldn't expect a typical woman to be strong enough to overpower someone and kill her like that."

"What if Mom was drunk or on drugs?"

"Did she often drink too much or take drugs?"

"No, and she was pretty fit and strong for her age. I can't imagine her being overpowered without putting up a fight unless she was already incapacitated in some way."

"A very good point. There was no sign she resisted her attacker."

"But why would she get drunk or take drugs with a stranger? She didn't know anybody from this area that I ever heard about."

"Maybe she ran into someone she knew, purely by accident . . . someone she would not have feared until it was too late."

"Yoo hoo, Edward!" Mrs. Davis was shouting at his front door. "Yoo hoo, Edward!"

"Out back," he yelled. Of course, he thought. Eileen had heard all about Felicia Jones's arrival from Willie, and she would be determined to meet the young woman and learn as much as she could. Mrs. Davis walked through the house and made her way to the dock. Callahan introduced the two women, trying to avoid giving away how annoyed he was that Mrs. Davis was inserting herself into a very private conversation—which had inspired him with a new thought about Hazel Jones's murder.

"I've made us all some sweet tea and ginger cookies," she said, as if she had been invited and everyone was expecting her to bring something. "I'm sure Miss Jones could use some refreshment after such a long trip."

"Thank you," Felicia replied. She glanced at Callahan and smiled a knowing smile, as if to say, I've seen this kind before.

Callahan was impressed with how easily the young woman caught on to Mrs. Davis and graciously played along. "The next thing you know, Eileen will be offering us dinner," he suggested—and instantly regretted.

Twenty-fourth

Without a word, Wingate turned and walked away. He clenched his fists and stamped his feet on the steel deck like a two-year-old. He hated having his schemes undone, and this last week seemed to have had more defeats than he was used to. Was he losing his touch? Despite the heat, he went and sat in his car and fumed for the remainder of the crossing. At the B&B he had selected for the night, he barely communicated with the owner despite her attempts to be warm and cheerful. He was raging and he couldn't stop. He didn't sleep well.

Whenever he had trouble sleeping, he often had a recurring, disturbing dream. He sat at the back of a courtroom watching Robert Jones sitting with his attorney. It appeared that everyone in the town of Greenville who could get off work had turned up at court. Word had gone out that the jury was returning with their verdict, and the room was humming with conversation as people filled every available seat and lined the walls. Dozens who couldn't get into the room were gathered at the door. The jury members filed into the courtroom. All had alligator heads. The judge said, "Have you reached a verdict?"

A very tall man with an especially large, blue alligator head stood up. Apparently he was the jury foreman. "We have, your honor." He paused and looked inquiringly at the judge, who nodded. "Guilty!" He shouted. In the dream, Wingate saw all eyes turn not toward Robert Jones but toward himself. He rose from his seat and tried to run from the courtroom, but his feet seemed glued to the floor. He waved his arms and shouted for help, but he could not move. At this point he usually woke up trembling and could not go back to sleep for fear the dream would recur.

Twenty-fifth

"Edward, you truly have a sixth sense. Dinner is exactly what I was going to propose." She nearly hopped up and down with excitement. "I knew that if it had been left to you, because you only have those deplorable frozen dinners in your house, you would have taken Miss Jones out somewhere, which is very civilized and kind, of course, but even the best restaurants are impersonal and noisy. We should all eat right here. The family that dines together stays together."

Callahan could barely control his anger at having his role as host co-opted by his neighbor. "We're a rather strange family, Eileen. Not one of us is related to any of the others."

"My dear Edward, if you only circulated in the community more, and didn't spend so much time on that project of yours, you'd know that, here on the Eastern Shore, we're all a family—even if we're not blood-related."

Felicia looked at Callahan. "You have a project? Am I keeping you from it?"

"It's nothing." Up to this moment, Callahan hadn't given any thought to the awkwardness of having a coffin in his shed and a young woman guest who came to collect her murdered mother's ashes. Now he was miserable.

"Edward is building a coffin for himself," said Mrs. Davis, clearly believing that another woman, even one a third her age whom she had only known for ten minutes, would agree with her that Callahan was too young and fit to be building a coffin.

Callahan tried to make light of it. "Never hurts to be prepared," he replied, instantly regretting his flippancy. He knew he was blushing. He wanted to punch Mrs. Davis, but instead said, "What do you say we go try your ginger cookies before the squirrels eat them."

* * *

After tea, Mrs. Davis proposed a cookout for their dinner. She had already made some potato salad and was going to make coleslaw and five-bean salad and bake some sweet potato biscuits. All Callahan had to do, she said, was to go to the local supermarket and buy ground beef and hot dogs, or if he liked, he could buy steaks, but she felt that was too fancy—the sort of thing come-heres would do, she said.

"But I *am* a come-here," said Callahan.

He invited Felicia to come along on his shopping trip, aiming to provide her with an opportunity to ask him more questions in private if she wished. She accepted, and the first question she asked after they were on their way was whether they could grill fish instead. She was a vegetarian, but ate fish occasionally to be sociable. Callahan knew he would enjoy this. It would be a little pushback against Mrs. Davis, something he was rarely quick enough to accomplish. They went to St. George Seafood and found a nice piece of rockfish. It was his favorite local seafood, so he bought enough so he could grill some for himself on another night.

At the supermarket a young man stopped them in the parking lot. "Do you use plastic bags when you shop?"

Felicia looked embarrassed, and said, "Not when I'm at home, but I'm visiting this area and didn't bring my cloth bags with me. I'm sorry." She looked anxiously at Callahan.

"I don't have any cloth bags either," he said, feeling embarrassed also, despite the fact that he'd never given any thought to shopping bags before.

"You can buy very nice cloth bags inside the store. You'll help save our local farmers' fields and equipment from the effects of plastic trash, and save marine animals like turtles from asphyxiation. It's so easy—simply avoid plastic and tell the store manager you want him to stop using plastic bags."

Felicia seemed surprisingly willing to discuss the merits of different kinds of grocery bags with the guy, so Callahan went in to shop alone. He only needed ground beef, a pack of hot dogs, rolls and buns, and sweet relish—and, of course, the cloth bags—so he expected he'd be out to rescue her in five or ten minutes. At the checkout line, which was much longer than he expected, he found himself standing behind Delbert Dix.

"Evening, Ed," he said. "Any progress in the investigation?"

"It's not my investigation, so I'm out of the loop."

"Well, then, let me tell you about a really good one that's sort of like the Hazel Jones case. I've been reading the local papers from the late nineteenth century on microfilm at the public library. There was this woman named Nellie Berard, whom the paper delicately described as 'being comely for her age and having known the favors of several local men.' In the winter of 1876 they found her body in a field a mile and a half from Port St. George. She had been hit on the head in four places with a blunt instrument. The newspaper article speculated that she had been killed elsewhere and dragged to the place in the field where she was found."

"No witnesses, I suppose."

"True, but she was seen walking between two houses the day before she was found in the field. The wife of the man who lived in one of the houses was being held in jail for further questioning because she was suspected of knowing more than she was telling."

"And?"

"Unfortunately, there were no more articles about this murder in the papers I've seen, so I have no idea how the story turned out."

"One thing I've noticed over the years, Delbert, is that when a woman is found dead like that, they rarely if ever successfully pin the crime on anyone. I hope the locals can do better with Mrs. Jones. Nobody deserves to die like that, and not having justice done only makes it worse."

When Callahan emerged from the store, with two newly purchased cloth bags for his groceries, Felicia and the young man were where he had left them, engaged in a lively conversation.

"Mr. Callahan," said Felicia, "I'd like you to meet my new friend, Monty Bergman."

The men shook hands. "I've noticed Monty out here before, but we've never been introduced."

"I'm not that surprised. No offense intended, but most people don't want to talk to me," said Monty. "They think I'm crazy for protesting about plastic bags, so they avert their eyes and walk on by. It's rare when somebody like Felicia comes along who really understands about threats to the natural environment."

"And, you know what?" said Felicia. "Monty and I have a connection."

"You've met before?"

"No, but the plastic bags they use here are made by Mom's old company—Dixiecraft Manufacturing in Greenville." She showed Callahan some fine print and a stylized miniature Confederate flag on the seam at the bottom of the bag. "Both my parents worked there at the time of my Dad's trial, and then Mom stayed on for a few years afterward."

Callahan felt old. He'd become accustomed to a life of routines and familiar people, a slow pace that suited him. Hazel Jones's murder seemed to have kicked his life into overdrive, and he was moving at an uncomfortable speed. Felicia had already invited Monty to join them at the cookout, and he had accepted, saying he would bring a six-pack of craft beer from Maryland as his contribution. Like Felicia, he didn't care for meat because, he explained at some length, modern meat production harms the environment and contributes to global warming.

At the cookout, Monty ate the extra rockfish Callahan had been planning to save for later. Callahan's annoyance about the loss of his fish was partially balanced by enjoying Mrs. Davis's irritation at having Felicia and her new friend take over the party. For her part, Mrs. Davis had invited Willie to stop by on his dinner break, and when he turned up, he irritated Callahan by not wanting to talk about anything except the progress of the investigation. Callahan felt that should be a forbidden topic while Felicia was present, but nothing could stop Willie's curiosity. Finally, Mrs. Davis insisted that Felicia not go to a motel, but stay overnight with her. By the time his house was finally empty and quiet, Callahan was exhausted.

A Coffin for Callahan

The next morning, he rose early and went to check on the bluebirds before breakfast. He saw the parents still flying in and out of the house at regular intervals and concluded they must be feeding some very hungry chicks. This was good news. He decided not to peek because the chicks might be almost ready to fly, but not quite. If startled, they are known to jump out of the nest onto the ground, where they become easy prey for cats or snakes as they flounder helpless in the grass. Doris had told him this a few years ago and, despite his lack of interest in birds at the time, the image of a struggling baby bird being swallowed by a six foot long black snake stuck with him.

He returned to the house and was pouring cereal into a bowl when Mrs. Davis rapped on his front door. "Good morning, Edward," she said as she brushed past him carrying a basket of steaming biscuits and a dozen eggs. "I'm here to make a hot breakfast for you and our honored guest. A good breakfast makes a good memory."

She continued, "That young lady is so delightful. We stayed up until two this morning talking about her life and work. She's bright as a button, yet so very friendly and easy to talk to. You'd never know she's from New York City."

"She was raised in South Carolina."

"Greenville. She told me all about it. Went to high school there and everything, which probably explains why she's so nice." Mrs. Davis had turned on Callahan's oven to keep the biscuits warm, found a bowl in his cupboard and begun scrambling eggs. "Do you have any jelly or marmalade, or do I need to go back and get mine?"

"I've got homemade blackberry jam from last year's Andrew Chapel sale that I never opened."

"Excellent, but now we need to talk." She pushed the bowl aside and sat down at Callahan's table.

"What about?"

"Felicia."

"She's okay isn't she?" Callahan suddenly began worrying.

"She's fine. She's taking a shower and getting dressed, but before she comes I want to talk about her love life."

"Eileen! That is none our business. She's in mourning. We have no right to start gossiping about her."

"She's making a big mistake, and it's all your fault."

"My fault?"

"You let her bring that Monty Bergman here yesterday. She's smitten, and he's terrible for her. He lives out in the woods somewhere by himself and all he does is agitate and propagandize about plastic bags and pollution. He doesn't have a job, and, in my opinion, he's careless about his appearance. My Willie is very sharp looking, has started a great career with the sheriff's office, and he's so polite and civilized. He would never stand out in front of a supermarket annoying people."

Callahan burst out laughing. "You're just griping because you were hoping Felicia would hook up with Willie."

"It's not that."

"Yes it is. You just want to be part of a little domestic drama—be a matchmaker. Come on, Eileen, give the kids a break."

"Sshh! I see her coming."

Twenty-sixth

Monday night was the slowest night of the week for poker, as Wingate knew well, but after his "clockwork victory," as he had dubbed it, he wanted some action to celebrate. Normally a cautious man, he occasionally felt an irrepressible urge to take a chance. On his way up the Garden State Parkway toward Atlantic City, he found himself getting more and more eager to be daring. It was a feeling he had learned to suppress—that same sense of invulnerability he'd experienced many years ago after his story about Robert Jones and the bookkeeper was swallowed whole by twelve South Carolina blockheads. If he couldn't suppress his urge to dare completely, at least he'd learned to direct it into expressions that were relatively harmless, like gambling. If he lost a few thousand dollars it was no big deal. He could afford it, and it was darn sight cheaper than getting into trouble with the law or being attacked by someone he'd cheated. In short, he'd learned to be careful when it mattered and reckless when it didn't. It was a skill he believed the rest of the human race should cultivate if they had any sense, which, in his view, they did not.

When he arrived at the Borgata, he checked in early and went for a quick lunch, followed by a haircut and a spa treatment. He liked being fussed over by strangers who didn't really care about him. It was flattering that they would do something so personal for money and it enhanced his feeling of superiority. Paying for personal grooming made much more sense to him than receiving such services from a friend or spouse who would expect something more than money in return.

A Coffin for Callahan

Late in the afternoon, poker was happening at only one table in the massive game room and all the players looked like permanent residents. He didn't see any easy money, so he moved on. He played blackjack for about an hour with an elderly Chinese couple and two young men from Florida sharing the table. Even though he wanted to take a risk, he couldn't entirely banish his instinct to make a buck. He played in a disciplined way and when he left the table he was thirty-five hundred dollars up. He was still looking for something risky and fun, but didn't see much going on in the huge casino that interested him. Out of sheer boredom, he sat down at a slot machine. These were loser traps, designed to suck money out of weak people with bad hearts and big rear ends, and he knew it, but he had a lucky feeling. Many people have such feelings and never win anything, but Wingate had the feeling and in forty minutes he was twenty-three hundred dollars ahead. The more he won, the stronger was his lucky feeling.

He moved to a hundred dollar machine. His lucky feeling never wavered even though he lost on the first five spins. On the sixth spin he won two thousand dollars. He was determined to exploit the feeling, and was loving the sense of being on the edge. On spin number eight he bagged eight hundred more. Now at more than five thousand dollars ahead for the day, he decided to take a real chance. He started doubling down his bets. After losing about three thousand dollars—but not a bit of his lucky feeling—he hit for fifteen thousand. Feeling appropriately rewarded for his perseverance and daring, he cashed out his ticket and demanded a room upgrade.

* * *

A Coffin for Callahan

Orion could not contain his joy at seeing his master entering the kennel to pick him up. In his excitement, he peed on the floor. Wingate mumbled an insincere apology, paid his bill, and led the eager animal to his car. They drove to the supermarket for some milk and other items, with Orion uncomfortably sharing the passenger seat with the blanket-wrapped base of the antique grandfather clock, which extended from the trunk to the dashboard through the fold-down back seat. At the supermarket, Wingate noticed Saturday's paper with the headline, BODY FOUND IN ST. GEORGE CREEK. The distractions of Atlantic City had kept his mind off Hazel Jones, but seeing the headline started him wondering.

As soon as he arrived home, he put away his groceries and released Orion into his run in the back yard. Then he went to his computer and checked the online version of the paper. An article scheduled to appear in Wednesday's print edition detailed the arrest of Filthy Pete, his release, and the arrest of Bullfrog Smith. Wingate's reacted by muttering, "Keystone Kops" to himself. The sheriff's office seemed to be floundering, which was exactly how he liked it. He had encountered inept police agencies before, and they were his favorite kind. The arrest of Bullfrog was encouraging, because Wingate's reading of history was that black men accused of raping and murdering white women were almost always convicted.

Twenty-seventh

Breakfast was almost the family affair Mrs. Davis claimed it should be until Felicia revealed that she was planning to drive out to see Monty Bergman's solar house and have lunch with her new friend. Mrs. Davis expressed her disapproval by muttering "to each his own," and inventing an excuse to retreat home. To pass the morning productively until the time for Felicia's departure, Callahan took his young visitor for a short walk around town, including showing her the wharf and Duck's Restaurant, where her mother's car had been abandoned.

"Didn't anybody at the restaurant see anything?"

"Willie told me the waiter and the bartender had conflicting stories about what your mother looked like, the clothes she was wearing, and whether she was alone or with a man, when she left, and several other details. The paper said the investigators concluded she had probably been at the restaurant, but they couldn't obtain any solid clues from the people they interviewed."

Felicia looked peeved. "Why didn't they check her credit card slip? That would tell them the exact time she left the restaurant."

"Maybe she paid cash."

"My mother never paid cash for things like dining out. She had one of those credit cards that tracked expenses by category. She used it for almost every purchase so she would have an annual breakdown of her expenses to compare against her budget."

Callahan looked out at the water. "Maybe somebody else paid her bill in cash because he didn't want to leave a record."

Felicia was crying. "That's it. I'll bet anything that's it. Damn it all, why is this happening to me again?" She leaned on Callahan's shoulder.

Instinctively, he put an arm around her and pulled her close. "Again?"

"Getting mixed up in another murder mystery. I spent my teenage years researching every detail of the murder my dad was accused of, trying to find evidence that would prove his innocence and get him released from jail. Now I'm playing amateur detective again. You may like investigating things, but I hate it."

"I'm sorry. Maybe we'd better go back."

"No. You seem to be more on the ball than the local people. Perhaps if I tell you the story, you can do better than them or me. I don't want my mom's killer to walk away as somebody walked away from killing Mrs. Lambert, leaving my dad to rot in prison."

They sat beside the boat ramp. "The person who was murdered, Mrs. Lambert, was the head bookkeeper at Dixiecraft, where Dad and Mom both worked. I didn't know her very well because I was a little child at the time, but I knew her teenage daughter Missy. Until she went to college, she was my babysitter whenever my parents had to work late or went to the movies or whatever. Missy's mom was working in the office after closing that night and somebody killed her there.

"A man named Charlie said he saw my father in the parking lot the night it happened. My father never denied it, so they convicted him. Mom never believed Charlie's story, and neither did I, but Dad refused to say whether he was there or whether he wasn't."

"And your dad never explained where he was if not at the office?"

"No. We used to visit him together, and sometimes Mom visited him alone. She said she often asked him to tell her the truth. She even told me that she suspected it involved another woman, and she told him that she didn't care if that was true, and he could tell her anyway, and she was ready to forgive him, but he never did."

"Does he know your mother is dead?"

"I called him as soon as I heard, but he'd already been told by the prison people, who saw it on the Internet."

"How did he take it?"

"He seemed detached and not interested in discussing her death or anything else. He's had periods of severe, prolonged depression in the past, and I'm afraid that may be starting again."

"Thanks for telling me. Now we'd better get you on your way to Monty's house."

With Felicia gone for a house tour and a promised home-made vegetarian quiche, Callahan decided the most practical way to use his free time was working on the coffin. He had finished all the sides, but at every joint between two pieces he needed to add a rib for strength. Six sides meant six joints, which called for six ribs. Each rib had to be ripped at an appropriate angle. For each of the three sets of corners—bottom, middle, and top—the angle differed. To be safe, he compared the angles on the plan to the measured angles between the sides. Fortunately, the angles in the coffin matched the angles on the plan. He ripped three pieces appropriately and cut them in half to make two ribs of each type. In less than an hour, he finished gluing them up and using screws to set them in place. He was surprised at his efficiency, and delighted with his good work.

* * *

The next day, returning from an early morning check on the bluebirds, Callahan noticed that Hazel Jones's little blue car was not in Mrs. Davis's driveway. He had wondered a little whether it was a good idea for Felicia to have gone away with Monty Bergman so soon after meeting him, and now his doubts turned to fears. He didn't have a phone number for either of them, and only had a vague idea where Monty lived. He thought of asking Mrs. Davis if she had heard anything, but decided that getting her involved would not help. As if his thoughts had somehow reached Felicia, his cell phone rang. She explained in hurried words that she had stayed over at Monty's house, but was now on her way into town. "When I called Mrs. Davis last night to tell her I wouldn't be coming to her house to stay, she sounded rather shocked."

"She would be."

"Actually, so am I, a little bit," Felicia added. "May we talk when I get back?"

Callahan couldn't say no, although he felt neither interested nor qualified to discuss Felicia's private life. On the other hand, she had no mother and her father was in prison, so who else could she talk to? It was his duty to play surrogate dad to this young woman, and he always did his duty. He collected his mail and put a fresh pot of coffee on. In a few minutes, Felicia knocked on his screen door.

"Come on in," he said.

"I hope I didn't worry you, running off like that. I've just had the most amazing experience."

"Slightly worried, maybe," said Callahan, understating his true feelings.

"I'm sorry. But I have a good excuse—I'm in love."

"Congratulations."

"It sounds silly doesn't it? I can't believe I've done this. I mean, I only met Monty yesterday—in a supermarket parking lot of all places—yet I instantly felt: he's the one. Do you think I'm going crazy?"

"You're young, not crazy."

"But impulsive you mean."

"Young people act. We old folks sit and cogitate until our time runs out and we keel over."

"I hope you don't think I sleep with every guy I meet."

"I hadn't got around to thinking that."

"Please don't think it of me, because I don't. In fact, I've never spent a night with anyone else except a man I dated for six months a couple of years ago. I don't do this sort of thing." She smiled. "But, then yesterday, I did."

"Love at first sight is a real thing." Callahan paused to take a sip of his coffee. "It happened to me."

"Thank you. Now I feel less like the only nut-case in the room."

"I fell in love with my Doris in about ten minutes. I helped her bring some groceries home, and by the time we reached her house I knew she was the one for me."

"That's lovely. But you probably didn't sleep over." She smiled again.

"Absolutely not. Doris lived with her mother and it was 1972. Things are different now."

"Mr. Callahan, would you hold me, please." She leaned forward with her arms outstretched, like a child wanting to be picked up.

Callahan pulled her close. "What's wrong?"

"I was just thinking how much I would love to tell Mom about Monty, and then I realized I can't tell her because she's dead, and then I realized if Mom hadn't been murdered, I never would have met Monty, so I wouldn't have anything to tell. What a mess!"

Callahan continued to hold Felicia close as she sobbed and shuddered. Although he had encountered many people in great emotional distress in his days on the police force, this situation was different. He felt responsible for Felicia, yet incapable of helping her. He hated the feeling. He felt incompetent. How could a man live for sixty years and not know how to help another human being in trouble? Fumbling for something constructive to say, he offered, "I know it's not the same thing, but perhaps you should call your dad."

"I'm not sure." She sat back in her chair and pushed her hair back. "He's had quite a shock, losing Mom. I'm not sure I could explain Monty and me in a way that wouldn't upset him more. I'm afraid of his depression."

"Well, for what it's worth, you've told me, and I'm very happy hearing your news."

"Thank you." She glanced at her watch. "I'd better go to Mrs. Davis's and change. I'm supposed to go pick up my mom's ashes at the funeral home at eleven."

"Hurry back. I know a good seafood place over in Wachapreague. I'll buy you lunch."

Twenty-eighth

Wingate spent the afternoon after his return from Atlantic City pulling weeds, trimming trees, and picking up dead branches. A stickler for an attractive garden, he'd done this many times before. However, this time he was also accumulating flammable materials while marking time until 4 p.m., when county fire regulations allowed outdoor fires. There's no point in attracting unwanted attention by lighting a blaze too soon, he reasoned. After everything burnable was in a big pile, he went into the house for some iced tea. Orion, who had been following him everywhere, came with him, uncharacteristically leaving the squirrels to themselves.

While there, Wingate took Hazel Jones's belongings out of his freezer. After carefully removing her keys, coins, rings, and other metal objects from her purse and clothing, he put the cloth and leather items, and Orion's rejected leash, as well as the plastic bag that had held her clothing after he stripped her body, into a pail lined with newspaper and poured in some paint thinner. He made a mental note that the metal items would need to be taken on a one-way boat ride soon. Orion sniffed the plastic bucket and went and sat in a corner. Amazing, Wingate thought, the little guy can smell death even through the odor of paint thinner.

After finishing his tea and confirming that it was after four o'clock, he took the bucket of clothing to the brush pile, stuffed it underneath, and lit it with his grill lighter. Almost immediately the pile roared into a ten-foot-high blaze. As the bonfire began to die down, Wingate methodically picked up unburned fragments of wood and weeds from around the edges of the pile and tossed them in to keep it going. He noticed with satisfaction that there seemed to be nothing left of Hazel Jones's belongings but ashes.

"Carter, what in hell are you doing?" said a loud voice behind him.

Wingate whirled, his face momentarily losing its color as his mind conjured the idea that he had been caught red-handed. Then he saw his neighbor, Monty Bergman, approaching across the lawn and calm returned. "Cleaning up my garden, Monty. What does it look like?"

"You're getting ashes and soot in the Chesapeake Bay, and the smoke from your bonfire is fogging up my solar glazing, reducing its efficiency."

"Tough luck, son, but fires like this are perfectly legal in Accomack County."

"Polluting the Bay isn't legal, and it's not necessary to burn this stuff. You could take it to a county convenience center to be chipped into mulch for organic gardening."

"I'm doing what I feel like doing. It's legal, and I'm on my own property. You, on the other hand, are trespassing. Go home and call the EPA if you don't like it."

Bergman walked a few steps away and turned. "This kind of irresponsible pollution is wrong, Carter, and you know it! I'll be exploring legal options."

"You do that," said Wingate, as his neighbor disappeared into the thick undergrowth separating their properties. "You just do that." For brief moment, Wingate wondered if the young man had noticed the bundle of Hazel's clothing he used to start the fire. Probably not, he concluded, but it still worried him a little. Later, as the fire died, he stirred the ashes carefully with a stick, spreading them around on the lawn as he went. He spotted a zipper and a button and picked them up. Back at his house, he added them to his sandwich bag of metal items.

* * *

Wingate's feeling of reassurance after incinerating evidence didn't last long. His morning mail included a copy of Friday's paper a day early, and newly reported developments in the Hazel Jones case weren't encouraging. First, Bullfrog Smith had been released without charge. Wingate's reliance on the racial bias of Virginia justice had failed him. Worse yet, a crabber checking his pots had recovered a concrete block with a length of frayed nylon line tied to it and reported it to the authorities. An avid reader of crime novels, the man had been following the Hazel Jones case in the papers with great interest. He had read about a nylon line being tied to her ankles, so when he found the concrete block with a similar line attached, he put two and two together. He recovered the hefty piece of evidence only a few hundred yards from Finley's Bar. This moved the location of the murder much closer to Wingate's house. He cursed to himself.

And, as if these two reversals of fortune weren't sufficient, the paper added that the sheriff had requested technical assistance from the Virginia Bureau of Criminal Investigation. Having gotten away with murder and uncountable lesser crimes, Wingate had little confidence in any police agency, but the BCI had far more resources than Accomack County, and if they threw enough of them at the problem, they might get lucky.

A Coffin for Callahan

Galloping anxiety began to take over. Working as a quickly as he could from memory, Wingate developed a short list of possible foreign escape locations. He would need to research their extradition treaties before making his final selection, but today he focused on the first step—flights to Panama, the foreign country he knew best and where much of his money resided. He found a flight on Aeromexico from Miami, which was an easy hop from Norfolk, his preference of the two nearest airports to the Eastern Shore. He'd used this route a few times before for his annual vacation. He booked a flight for July seventh, with a return ticket for two weeks later that he had no intention of using. He could have flown sooner, but he needed time to prepare the most valuable of his antiques for shipment out of the country. It was a risky compromise between safety and wealth preservation, and he didn't like compromises. Although a lot could happen in six days, he did not want to lose the value of the personal possessions in his house. He'd spent years accumulating them, and the amount of money involved was considerable. He was especially irritated about the grandfather clock. The pearls may not have been worth much, but they were a lot easier to carry than a seven-foot-tall clock.

He banged his fist on the dining room table. Why did that stupid Jones woman have to show up in Port St. George anyway? If she hadn't appeared, he wouldn't have had to kill her, and his life could have gone on as before. (He could have asked himself why he approached her in Duck's restaurant and introduced himself, but it was not in Carter Wingate's nature to find fault with his own behavior.)

Then he glanced out the window. On the creek, not two hundred yards from the shore, was Monty Bergman in his puny plastic kayak, staring back at Wingate's house through binoculars. The sneaky little shit! What does he think he's doing? Then Wingate noticed a pair of snowy egrets feeding on the edge of the marsh. Doesn't that boy ever get sick of looking at the damned birds? Wingate let Orion out the door, knowing he would run to the edge of the marsh and scare the birds away.

As he watched his Scottie run gleefully toward the two white feeders, Wingate realized with regret that, by deciding to leave the Eastern Shore for good, he had lost his chance to pay Monty back for buying the property next door. Then, while watching Orion bounding back and forth, the birds taking flight, and Monty putting his binoculars aside and starting to paddle farther down the creek, he suddenly thought of a superb method of revenge—and it might pay big dividends.

Monty Bergman spends far more time on the creek than I do, he thought. All the neighbors know he lives alone and has no girlfriend and that he's a bit nutty and a loner. He doesn't come from the Eastern Shore, but from the big city of Chicago, so nobody particularly likes him. He's annoyed the sheriff's office with his protests and aggressive petitioning in front of stores, so they probably would love an excuse to lock him up. Wingate went through his old newspapers and found the county's number for anonymous crime tips.

Twenty-ninth

When they returned from Wachapreague, Felicia asked if she could cook a meal at Callahan's house. "I'd like to have Monty over. I owe him—and you—some hospitality, and I'd like you to get to know him better. He's very unusual, but an extremely cool guy."

"Sounds like fun." Callahan was pleased that he would have an opportunity to study Monty more closely. Although he had never had a daughter of his own to watch grow to maturity, he seemed to be experiencing paternal feelings for Felicia. He would make a world of trouble for anyone who hurt her, including, if necessary, Monty Bergman.

Felicia called, but her face took on a puzzled, then horrified, expression as she spoke on her phone. The color drained out, and lines appeared that Callahan had never noticed before. "Thank you," she said in a whisper, and put the phone on the kitchen table.

"What's wrong?"

"Monty's been arrested. I spoke to a guy named Andy, who says he's Monty's lawyer. He's at the house feeding the dog and locking up."

"Come on! Even in Accomack County they must have better things to do than arresting people for picketing the supermarket."

"They've arrested him for killing my mother."

"When?"

"This morning about ten. It couldn't have been more than a few minutes after I left his house."

Callahan was speechless. Anger was building in him in a way that he hadn't experienced in years.

"This can't be!" Felicia buried her face in her hands. Tears flowed.

Callahan felt useless. He tried to think of something comforting to say, but all he could come up with were platitudes about hoping for the best and being patient. He barely knew this young woman, and he knew even less about her new boyfriend. Was it possible that Monty Bergman really killed her mother? If so, it was sickening to think that Felicia had fallen in love with him. But why would Monty Bergman kill Hazel Jones?

Mrs. Davis rapped on the screen door. "Edward, are you home?"

"Yes, Eileen, in a moment." Shit, he thought. What a time for her to show up!

"Oh, dear, Felicia. What's the matter, honey? Did that boy upset you?"

Felicia looked at Mrs. Davis. "No."

"He's been arrested, Eileen, for killing Mrs. Jones."

"And you stayed over at his house last night. How perfectly horrible. No wonder you're upset."

"He didn't do it."

"The sheriff's office wouldn't arrest him if they didn't have evidence."

Callahan surprised himself by nearly shouting at Mrs. Davis, "They've already arrested two people who had nothing to do with Mrs. Jones's murder, so how do you know this isn't their third dumb mistake?"

"You're the investigator, Edward. You explain it."

At this point, to Callahan's delight, the investigative part of his brain, so long dormant, finally awoke. Ignoring Mrs. Davis, he asked "Felicia, does Monty own a boat?"

"A kayak. He uses it for bird watching."

"How about some other boat?"

"No. He told me it's unethical for a single person to have more than one of anything, so if he wanted another boat he would have to sell the kayak."

"And how big is the kayak?"

"Not very. When I was there, he said he would like to take me out on the creek, but it only holds one. He said it would be very dangerous with two."

"Please forgive me, but I'm going to ask some difficult questions and say some things that may hurt." He paused, and Mrs. Davis, clearly interested and not wanting to miss anything, took a chair at the kitchen table as if she had been invited. "How much did your mom weigh?"

"I don't know. She was not as tall as me, but a little chubbier, so maybe about the same weight—one hundred and fifteen to one hundred and twenty pounds."

"And Monty? Do you know how much he weighs?"

"He's pretty skinny, because he doesn't eat any meat or processed foods, but still, he probably weighs more than me."

"My guesstimate, from seeing him when he was here, would be one-fifty to one-sixty."

"That sounds about right."

Mrs. Davis moved in her seat. "What does Monty Bergman's weight have to do with whether he's a murderer or not?"

"Keep listening, Eileen, and all will become clear." Callahan rose from his seat and went outside. He returned with a concrete block, one of several that for years had been stacked in a loose pile under his back porch. "Back in a minute," he said, and went into the bathroom. He came back and passed through the kitchen without speaking, took the block back outside, and returned to the kitchen. "Thirty-eight pounds."

Felicia smiled. "Now I see it."

"Whoever killed your mother took her body, a concrete block similar to this one, and himself out into the creek in some kind of boat." Callahan took a marker and wrote the numbers for the weights of Mrs. Jones, Monty, and the concrete block on the DORIS'S DAILY LIST white board, which up to today he had never used. "Two hundred and ninety-three pounds. Add seven for a paddle, rope, and maybe a life jacket, and you have an even three hundred. That's a lot of weight for a small kayak."

"How much can a kayak hold?"

"It probably varies with the brand and size of the kayak, but I've heard they have weight ratings on the nameplate, so we could find out."

"I'll go look." Felicia jumped from her chair and without a word left the house.

As the sound of her car faded, a bewildered Mrs. Davis said, "Youth, it's wasted on the young."

"I don't believe she's wasting anything, Eileen. Give her a chance."

Expecting that Felicia would be home in a little while, and recalling how distressed she had been, he went to the bakery with the aim of picking out something sweet to lift her spirits. Now that she would not be cooking dinner for Monty, and "the family" as Mrs. Davis persisted in calling their foursome, the two of them would probably have to eat out again or accept something homely that they concocted together. It promised to be a somber meal.

At the bakery, he found Delbert Dix sitting at a table alone, with a large pile of photocopies from old newspapers spread out around him. "Hello, Ed, how's it going?"

"Could be better." Callahan explained about Monty being arrested. Then asked, "Taking another day off?"

"Yeah, the warm weather we've been having has discouraged folks from topping up their propane. They'll probably be sorry this fall when prices go up." He riffled through his papers. "Hey, want to hear about a good murder?"

"I'm up to here with Hazel Jones, but maybe you can shed some light on the subject."

"I'm not sure about that, but the news story I've just been reading involved killing a woman. There were actually two possible motives for this murder. Perhaps one of them applies in Hazel Jones's case. It was like this. There was this tugboat captain named Robert Murphy who, in his forties, married a seventeen-year-old girl. It was his second marriage, his first wife having died."

"Natural causes?"

"The paper didn't say, so I suppose so. Anyhow, when he married his teenaged second wife, the couple first lived in Norfolk where Captain Murphy commanded a tugboat. Later they moved to Melfa, here on the Eastern Shore. Then, while her husband was out on his tugboat—and the paper doesn't say why—Mrs. Murphy took their four-year-old son and moved home to Chincoteague. Both she and her husband were originally from the island. She began to socialize with young friends of hers that she had known before marrying the captain, and apparently was very popular in the town. This irritated her husband, who by this time had returned from his work. He stayed on Chincoteague more than a month, even though he was supposed to go back to Norfolk to be on the tugboat. Apparently, at least according to local gossip reported by the newspaper, he was becoming very jealous of his wife and her socializing. In addition, there was also this guy, Victor Chase, with whom Mrs. Murphy had apparently had some kind for relationship before she married the captain. Chase, who had been away somewhere, returned to Chincoteague not long before her death. There was testimony at Murphy's trial that the captain was afraid his wife was going to desert him to take up with this Chase guy again.

"Then, as if all that wasn't enough, along comes an insurance check for three hundred dollars for Mrs. Murphy, because her brother had died in France in the First World War. She wanted to spend the money on a new Easter outfit, but her husband said she should give the check to him instead so he could pay the balance due on some furniture they had stored in Norfolk. She said she would give him half the money, but not all. This seems to have been the immediate cause of his action.

"When she refused to hand over the check, he shot her. She was killed by one bullet that entered her right side under the arm and came out on the left side. After shooting his wife, Captain Murphy picked her up off the floor and seated her in a chair. He returned the pistol to the person he'd borrowed it from, and then went to his father's house where he said a doctor was needed because he'd shot his wife. "

"Pretty gruesome. What happened to him?"

"He was tried and convicted of second degree murder. He received eighteen years in the penitentiary in Richmond."

"I'd be surprised if either love or money had anything to do with Hazel Jones's death, but thanks anyway for the good story. I'd better get back."

As Callahan opened the front door, the phone was ringing. It was Willie Custis, Jr.

"What's up, Willie?"

"Just thought I'd let you know the sheriff has got a really good suspect under arrest in the Hazel Jones killing. It's that environmentalist guy, Monty Bergman, who was at your cook-out."

"I know." He could almost hear Willie's disappointment in the silence on the line.

"Oh, uh, okay. But let me tell you why. It turns out he lives out near Finley's Bar, which is close to where that waterman found the concrete block anchor. He also wrote a newsletter a few months ago where he said that Dixiecraft Manufacturing is top of his list of most hated polluters because they make plastic shopping bags."

"So?" Callahan was becoming angry, but he let Willie continue in the hope he would say something useful.

"Well, it turns out that Mrs. Jones used to work for Dixie-craft Manufacturing."

"Willie, I know that, too. Take a moment and think. Hundreds of people probably worked for Dixiecraft Manufacturing at one time or another, and as far as we know Monty Bergman hasn't tried to kill any of them. Why pick on an ex-employee, who just happened to be driving through this area on her way home, and kill her over work she did years ago?"

"I don't know."

"I'll tell you something else you probably don't know. Monty Bergman only owns one boat—a small kayak—and there is no way he could have used that to float a body and a concrete block anchor out into the creek. He couldn't have put Mrs. Jones's body in St. George Creek if he'd wanted to, which he didn't because he didn't kill her."

"Wow! I hadn't thought of the kayak angle. You're really investigating the way they told us at the academy. I'll pass this information along."

"Willie! Write your thoughts on a piece of paper and slip it under their door—and don't sign it. Your helpful hints are going to kill your career."

Thirtieth

With his departure plans beginning to take shape, Carter Wingate felt good. He'd been anxious before, but now he felt that it was time to savor his last few days on the Eastern Shore. When Wingate was in a particularly good mood, as he was today, he liked to take Orion for a walk along the creek-front road he shared with his neighbors. He decided to take Orion for this longer than usual walk to give the little dog a final encounter with of some of his favorite haunts.

Wingate's house was one of several set along the edge of the creek. All of them shared a driveway that extended about a mile from the main road toward St. George Creek and terminated in a T-junction a few yards from the water. To the right was Wingate's four acres of mainly wooded ground—the surviving remnant of a plantation house constructed in 1768. To the left was Monty Bergman's small lot, and beyond that half a dozen other houses of varying sizes and conditions. Wingate didn't like any of the neighbors, so he was happiest when nobody was outside to speak to, which was usually the case.

Needless to say, Orion was excited whenever the opportunity arose to take this longer walk. He strained at his leash and didn't behave very well in his excitement when he realized today was a long walk day. Wingate was in no hurry, so he let Orion sniff to his heart's content among the leaves and brush lining the road. They walked past Monty's, and then past the Browns' rather pompous three story, eight bedroom beach house and the Savitches' mobile home, past a couple of small, weather beaten cottages owned by two related families from New York who rarely visited, past the converted fisherman's shanty with handmade tile floors and chef's kitchen, and past the ultramodern, metal-sheathed cube that an architect from Richmond had built for his daughter and son-in-law four months before they divorced. The road dead-ended on a small beach, which Orion enjoyed immensely—running and checking out every hole and piece of smelly debris along the tide line.

After a while, Wingate began to feel the heat of the afternoon sun. Orion didn't seem to mind, but his master craved an iced tea and air conditioning. As they approached Monty Bergman's house, a small blue car approached them very rapidly and turned into Monty's drive. As they passed the house, Wingate saw a young woman get out of the car. Except for being slightly thinner and taller, she looked exactly like Hazel Jones. The car had a South Carolina tag. It was Hazel Jones's car. His calm shattered, Wingate hurried the startled Orion home.

Once inside his house, he started thinking. He remembered that Hazel had had a daughter about four or five years old at the time of Robert Jones's trial. This would be she. But how in hell did she get involved with Monty Bergman? What does it mean? Of course, she would never recognize me after all these years, he thought, or would she? Having Hazel's daughter next door was something he'd never expected, and he didn't like it.

Thirty-first

When Callahan returned from the bakery, Felicia was sitting on his porch, playing with a small dog. "Did you find him, or did he find you?" he asked, chuckling.

"Neither. He's Monty's. His name is Thoreau. Andy, the lawyer, said he didn't have time to go out to Monty's house a couple of times a day to feed him and take him for walks, so I brought him home with me."

Callahan smiled at the thought that Felicia considered his house her home also. It felt good. The small mongrel sniffed at Callahan's feet, then went to sit next to Felicia's chair. "So what about the kayak?"

"I looked all over before I found it, and I'm not sure if it's the right thing. There was a sticker inside where nobody would ever notice it that said the maximum displacement was two hundred and fifty-five pounds."

"That settles it, then. Monty could not have killed your mother. If he had loaded himself, her body, and the cinder block onto that kayak, he would have sunk like a rock."

"So why has the sheriff picked on him?"

"Anybody's guess. Does Monty have an alibi?"

"He does, but I'm not sure if I should say. It's kind of a secret."

"When Willie Custis called, he said he's going to forward the kayak info to the investigators, but I wouldn't count on that doing the trick. You'd better tell me the alibi."

"I should really ask Monty first."

"Then history's repeating itself."

"I don't understand."

134

"Monty's behaving exactly as your father did in his time. He has a good alibi, but he won't tell anyone what it is. Monty could end up in prison the same way."

"Seriously?"

"Nuttier things have happened. These investigators are desperate. The public wants results. Politicians want results. The county has arrested two people who couldn't be charged for lack of evidence. There's not much evidence against Monty either, but if he doesn't talk, they'll likely treat his silence as proof of guilt and try to prosecute."

"I'll have to ask Monty."

"Felicia, do not forget. This is not only about Monty. There's a murderer out there somewhere—a man who killed your mother. If Monty doesn't talk and goes to prison, his stubbornness sets that guy free, the same as when your father wouldn't talk. What sounds like a noble act—keeping your mouth shut and going to prison, probably to protect someone else—gives a free pass to a murderer."

"Okay, if you'll promise not to tell the investigators or anybody . . ."

"God help me!" Callahan pounded his fist on the table and stood up. "We've got to talk to your father."

"But he doesn't know anything about Monty and me."

"Felicia, listen. I've finally seen how this works. The guy who killed your mother is probably the same man who killed the bookkeeper years ago. Your mother must have bumped into him somehow and confronted him. Maybe he's changed his identity and started a new life. Her discovery of him would have ruined everything. He killed her to silence her."

"So what has my father got to do with it?"

"We need to get him to tell the truth so we can find the real murderer, because that person, whoever and wherever he is, is the person who killed your mom."

"I'll call the prison and say it's an emergency." Felicia pulled her phone from her bag. After a few minutes, first with the prison front desk, then with the warden's secretary, and finally with her father, she said, "He won't talk over the phone."

"Where's your dad incarcerated?"

"Perry Correctional Center. It's in a small town called Pelzer."

"How far from here?"

"It's around five hundred miles to Greenville, and Pelzer's another twenty or so. Maybe five hundred and twenty miles?"

"Go to Mrs. Davis's and pack your stuff."

In less than an hour, which would have been sooner without Mrs. Davis's protests and insistence that she make them ham sandwiches, coleslaw, and sweet tea for the journey, Callahan and Felicia were on their way south—with Thoreau in the car since Mrs. Davis's hospitality did not extend to looking after a dog—even though it would have been a big favor to Callahan and therefore put a huge IOU to Eileen in his debt bank.

Crossing the Bay through the Bridge-Tunnel was easy and, unusually for a Saturday afternoon, Norfolk area traffic wasn't bad. They ate their sandwiches while driving U.S. 58 toward Emporia. At the first fuel stop, Callahan suggested they go another couple of hours to High Point and find a motel. "That'll give us less than four hours to go in the morning," he said. "I'd be surprised if they'll let anybody in before noon."

A Coffin for Callahan

At breakfast, Callahan asked, "Are you ready to tell me Monty's alibi?"

"I want to ask him first."

"If you do, he'll probably say no. You said your mom asked your father to tell and he always refused. This is different. You know the story, and you can act."

"He's trying to protect some friends, not himself."

"Very honorable, but would they do the same for him?"

"I don't know."

"My guess is not. Most people look out for number one."

"Do we need the alibi to get Monty out?"

"Not if we can identify the real killer. We need Monty's alibi now to show your dad how holding onto a secret can hurt people you care about."

"In this case, telling the secret could hurt people, too."

"That's probably the case with your dad's alibi also. Is what Monty was doing illegal?" Callahan took a sip of his coffee.

"Yes."

"Drugs?"

"Yes."

"Dealing?"

"Nothing like that! He and a group of his friends were rolling joints and packaging them in sandwich bags to give to cancer patients and others with chronic pain. One of them grows the marijuana and the rest distribute it to people they know who need some. It's kind of like a club."

"When did this happen?"

"From late in the afternoon until about midnight on the day before you found my mom."

"At Monty's?"

"No, . . . at the friend's house, in a place called Hopeton. I don't know where that is."

"It's nowhere near Monty's or St. George Creek, but we should avoid giving the drug squad an early Christmas present if we can help it. They'd love to bust a whole gang of people in one swoop—especially if they're do-gooder come-heres."

"So we need to get Dad to talk to save Monty."

"Yes." He drained his cup. "Ready?"

* * *

The Perry Correctional Institution was nowhere near Pelzer. In fact, it was distinguished by being nowhere near anywhere. Set in a lightly populated area of small farm fields and woods, it sprawled across a manufactured wasteland surrounded by two fences, both of which were topped with concertina wire and studded at intervals with CCTV cameras. Callahan recognized the design. "This place is maximum security. What's your dad doing here?"

"He's classified as a violent offender because of the nature of his crime."

Obtaining access was surprisingly easy. The prison staff was well aware of Robert Jones's depressive nature and the recent loss of his wife. They seemed relieved that a family member had come to visit. Clearly, they didn't want an embarrassing suicide on their hands. Callahan's Philadelphia FOP Lodge retiree ID card was his entry ticket, conferring upon him trusted status. They were told Jones was finishing lunch and would be brought to see them soon.

The reception area, with its divided interview stalls and bulletproof glass, reminded Callahan of a cow barn. Each animal gets a stall facing another animal in the opposite stall. After a few minutes in which they waited in silence, absorbing the efficient gloom of the place, a guard led Robert Jones into the stall opposite them and then took a seat in a chair a few steps behind his prisoner. Jones was thinner and shorter than Callahan had imagined him. It was clear that Felicia took after her mother and not her dad. Nothing physical about him appeared to have been expressed in his daughter. His eyes were brown; hers were blue. He was small boned and frail looking; she was broad shouldered for a woman and looked strong. His ears stuck out awkwardly; hers were small and well formed.

Jones seemed unmoved by his daughter's presence and exchanged only a few conventional words of greeting, almost as if he were meeting a couple of social workers rather than his daughter and her friend. "How are you feeling, Daddy?" Felicia asked.

"Okay. Kinda down about your mother, naturally, and I've been having trouble sleeping for the past few days, but I'm okay."

"This is my friend Ed Callahan."

Jones barely moved and avoided eye contact. "Hello, Ed," he said. His mouth and eyes were expressionless.

"Pleased to meet you, Robert. I'm very sorry about Mrs. Jones."

Felicia went directly to the subject of their visit, but when she tried to explain about her love for Monty and how his behavior when arrested resembled that of her father, she began to cry and couldn't continue, so Callahan explained the situation. As he spoke, Robert Jones sat impassively, clearly listening, but also clearly intending to contribute nothing and make Callahan do all the work. After an explanation about Monty and his friends and the marijuana, and noting the similarity between Monty's behavior and Jones's, Callahan asked Jones to give up the story of what he was doing the night of the murder. He refused.

"Then please tell me, were you or were you not at the plant that night?"

"I'm not prepared to say."

"You may not be, but I am. You were not at the plant. You were cheating on your wife and you're remaining silent to protect the other woman." Felicia gasped, and Callahan felt dirty for using cop-like behavior in front of her, but he was becoming enraged at Jones.

"No."

"If you didn't do that, then you must have killed the bookkeeper."

"No."

"Yes, you did. The jury said so, and they were right."

"I never killed anyone."

"You did, Mr. Jones, yes you did, whether you killed that poor bookkeeper or not. Your silence killed your wife Hazel, and whether you help me find her killer or not, I'm going to prove you're as responsible for her death as the son-of-a-bitch who strangled her."

A Coffin for Callahan

Jones stood up and pounded on the glass with his fists, opening his mouth as if to speak, but with no sound coming out. Felicia ran from the room, and the guard grabbed Jones and hustled him out the back door, ending the interview.

Why did I do that? Callahan wondered. Feeling intense remorse at Felicia's reaction (but not particularly sorry about her father's), he went to find her. She stood in the hallway not far from the interview room, gazing glassy eyed out the window, but she didn't appear to have been crying, which surprised Callahan. He said, "Please forgive me. I got carried away."

"You were only doing your best to help. My father has always been like that since Mrs. Lambert's murder. He never responded to me or my mother's questions and pleading. It's as if he doesn't care at all what happens to his family."

"I'm sure he cares." Callahan actually wasn't sure, but this seemed to be the right thing to say. "He seems to be seriously troubled, but won't seek help or open up to people. It's a shame he's our only link to that night."

She smiled. "I wish I were older."

So relieved was he by that smile that he began to tear up. "If you were my age, you'd never say that."

"I don't mean to wish my life away, but if I were older now, I would have been older then, so I might know something useful."

"Do you remember anything?"

"Not about the day of the murder or the trial, but I recall little bits from later in my childhood. For instance, when I was in first or second grade, I remember a big argument my mother had with my grandmother. My grandmother—my dad's mother—always supported Dad's silence, saying he must have his reasons. Mom was struggling to keep a roof over our heads and pay legal bills on one small salary. She believed Dad was innocent and that his refusal to talk was responsible for her situation. My grandmother said it was unfair to blame what happened on Dad. She asked why Mom didn't blame Charlie Walton, who was the guy who testified he saw Dad the night of the murder, or Missy Lambert."

"What did Missy Lambert have to do with it?"

"I'm not sure. She wasn't in town the night her mother was murdered. She was at college. Now she's married with kids. She and her husband are both preachers."

"What about Walton?"

"He moved away not long after the trial, my mother said, and she was very bitter about it. She said he did his dirty work—testifying against Dad, and then ran off. She never believed his story."

"Can we speak to Missy?"

"I suppose so, but why?"

"Sometimes a person will cough up a small detail that they don't regard as important, but makes a big difference in our understanding of a crime. I'd very much like to know why your grandmother mentioned Missy's name."

Thirty-second

The next day Wingate woke in a state of agitation. He had not slept well, and he felt like a rabbit sensing that a fox was near. Rising from his bed, he pulled the curtain back slightly and peeked out, as if expecting to see someone watching him. His instinct for self-preservation was kicking in, and past experience had taught him to go with it. Acting to protect himself always made him feel better.

As a first step, he decided not to deposit the wad of cash he had collected after his exceptional run at the casino. It would make a handy reserve for emergencies. After a quick breakfast and a walk around his property with Orion, he settled down at his computer. He checked the status of his foreign bank accounts and satisfied himself that he had enough to live on for several years. His many successes at fleecing the clueless elderly had yielded a significant fortune. Wherever possible, he obtained his profits in cash, and he had been careful to set up bank accounts in Panama, Luxembourg, and Singapore. He made regular deposits by visiting Panama about once a year to add to the two accounts he maintained there. Later, he would transfer money online from one or the other of these accounts to the accounts in the other two countries, neither of which he had ever visited or planned to. Carter Wingate was smart, and he had realized early in life that smart people who pursue their dreams aggressively tend to accumulate enemies. He had been careful to make certain that none of his enemies—or the tax man—would ever enjoy a piece of his fortune.

Concerning where his future home should be, he reasoned that, if he avoided popular, expensive locations he could live decades without the need to work or do business. Retiring from business would help him stay below police radar. In any case, he would never choose to reside in an expensive place like London or Paris, because they were too connected to the outside world, and besides, they had too many people. The type of place he wanted would be relatively unpopular, but have sufficient American, Canadian, or British expatriates so he wouldn't stand out as the only rich, English-speaking white guy in the neighborhood. Clearly, he would need to do a bit more online research.

Thirty-third

Felicia remembered that Missy Lambert and her husband preached at a large church somewhere outside Greenville. A quick search of the web on her phone—a procedure that bewildered Callahan, who still used a flip phone he'd bought at Walmart years before—located the Green Pastures Endless Love Church in Renfrew. According to its web site, it was the spiritual home for more than five thousand souls. At the top of the list of seven pastors were Thomas T. Lee and Melissa Jane Lee, co-senior pastors. After the short drive from Greenville to Renfrew, Felicia and Callahan were proceeding slowly up a winding approach road lined with small magnolia trees. "This thing is bigger than a basketball arena," said Callahan.

"They like their churches huge here," Felicia replied, smiling.

"Have you kept in touch with Missy?"

"Not really. We exchanged Christmas cards for a few years and she may still be connected to my LinkedIn page, but that's about it."

They parked in the mall-sized lot and went inside the church. The two-story atrium foyer of the church resembled the front lobby of a corporate office or a contemporary art museum, with a semi-circular low counter upon which there were four computer screens. The ceiling was at least two stories high and the wall colors were bright gold, blue, and green. It was unlike any church Callahan had ever been in. At first there appeared to be nobody around and Callahan wondered if they should have called first. He was about to apologize for leading Felicia on a wild goose chase, and suggest they try another time, when a girl of sixteen or seventeen appeared as if from thin air. "May I help you?" Her floor length polka dot dress was a brilliant violet and lime green that made Callahan's eyes hurt.

"I'm Felicia Jones and this is my friend Ed Callahan. We were hoping to speak with Missy... I mean Reverend Mrs. Lee."

The girl threw her arms around Felicia. "We were so sorry to hear about your mom. Mommy and Daddy held a special family service and we all prayed for her."

Freed from the young girl's hug, Felicia said, "You're Missy's daughter?"

"That's right. I'm Abigail, eldest of five."

"You look very much like your mother did when she was my babysitter. I'm delighted to meet you."

Callahan said, "Is your mother available? We'd really like to speak to her if possible."

Abigail went behind the counter and picked up a phone. After a few brief words with someone, she said. "Mommy and Daddy will meet you in the Memory Garden. Please follow me."

The teenager led them through a labyrinthine series of hallways, meeting rooms, classrooms, and offices until they found themselves in a garden carved out of the building itself. This large green space consisted mainly of conifers trimmed and lighted to look like Christmas trees, with walkways edged with flowers in various bright, cheerful colors. Plastic benches in shades as brilliant as the flowers were placed in nooks along brick walkways. The space was delightfully cool. Callahan looked up and realized that the entire garden was under a dome—protected from the natural elements and air conditioned. No birds, insects, or other animals were to be seen or could get in to spoil the perfection of this man-made Eden. After a few more turns on the winding path, they arrived at the center of the garden. Beside a small pool with orange and white koi swimming under lily pads was a gazebo with chairs and a table. An impeccably dressed man and woman were sitting at the table. They rose in unison and smiled warmly. Abigail introduced them as her parents.

"Call me Reverend Tommy."

"Call me Reverend Missy."

"Pleased to meet you," said Callahan. "Call me Ed."

The adults all shook hands, which seemed to Callahan normal enough for the men, but after Abigail's warm response upon meeting Felicia, he was puzzled at her mother's reserve. In contrast to her daughter, Missy made no effort to hug Felicia, and shook her hand quickly and efficiently. The two pastors offered condolences in a practiced manner and said they would be praying for Hazel.

"So what brings you to us?"

Felicia offered a quick summary of what had happened since her mother's death, including the arrest of Monty and their lack of success talking to her father. "Since Reverend Missy is the only adult we know other than my Dad who's still living in this area, we would like to ask you some questions about the night your mom was killed."

Reverend Tommy spoke quickly, "Abigail, this sounds like it's going to be a very grown-up conversation. Perhaps you'd better go back to working on that children's program."

"Yes, Daddy." She rose and marched away. Her body language suggested she was not happy to be excluded, but she was clearly accustomed to obeying her parents.

"What do you wish to know?" Reverend Missy smoothed her long, light blue skirt as if she were preparing to be photographed, and then folded her hands in her lap.

"Mr. Jones refused to tell us what he was doing the night of your mother's murder . . . ."

"I was not there, so I don't know what he was doing either."

"Of course, I understand that." Callahan was beginning to feel glad he chose to question Missy Lambert Lee. "You were at college?"

"I was on my way home from college that night for a weekend break, but I had car trouble. My Mom's car also was not working, and I was supposed to pick her up at her office at Dixiecraft on my way home. If I had not had car problems, she would probably be alive today."

"I'm sorry. That must be a terrible burden to bear."

"True, but it's in the past. In our ministry we urge people to put the past in its proper place, because whatever happened in those times is what God ordained, even if we don't understand why. We encourage our church members to focus on the future and build new lives from the ruins of old ones. I take my own advice."

Reverend Tommy interjected, "Our faith is grounded in love and prayer. We believe God recognizes those who love him and his only begotten son Jesus and rewards them according to the love they have and the sincerity of their prayers.

Dwelling on the past pulls a person away from love and prayer. In fact, it could even be construed as questioning God's will."

"My apologies for dwelling on the past, but one last question: do either of you ever see or speak to Mr. Robert Jones?"

"No," the couple answered in unison.

Callahan thanked them for their time and rose to leave. The Pastors Lee offered to show them out of the church, so together they went back through the extensive building. Callahan walked with Reverend Tommy, exchanging small talk about sports, and Felicia walked silently beside Reverend Missy. At the front door they shook hands again. Callahan asked, "By the way, Reverend Missy, what was the matter with your car?"

Reverend Missy stared at him for a moment as if he had punched her, but soon recovered her composure and smiled. "It ran out of gas and I had to hitchhike twenty miles to the next town to buy some."

In the extensive empty parking lot, they found Abigail, playing with Thoreau. "On my way back to my desk, I heard him barking, and he looked so sad cooped up in the car, I just had to let him come out to play. I hope you don't mind."

"Not at all," said Felicia. "I was thinking of giving him a run before we started driving again, so you've done us a nice favor."

"He's so cute. Have you had him long?"

Felicia explained about Monty being in jail and how she and Callahan had ended up responsible for Thoreau. The story of a lover in jail for a crime he didn't commit touched Abigail deeply, and she began to cry. "What if they convict him and he never gets out of jail? What will you do?"

Felicia put her arm around Abigail's shoulders. "He'll get out, because Mr. Callahan will keep digging until he finds the truth, which will set Monty free."

"John, chapter 8, verse 32," said Abigail.

"Exactly," said Felicia.

The conversation between the two young women blossomed, leaving Callahan to watch the birds and wonder how his own bluebirds were doing. He found it interesting to hear a female friendship develop as if he were not there.

Felicia asked about the children's project Abigail was working on. It turned out to involve folded paper puppets that represented the animals in Noah's ark. They were designed to look like simple flat squares of paper, but when unfolded they became recognizable lions, tigers, bears, elephants, and horses.

"That's very spatially sophisticated. Where did you learn it?"

"I invented it. I enjoy designing things like that."

"What a cool coincidence! I do similar things—not with paper animals, but with minimalist recyclable packaging for consumer products—for my industrial design job in New York."

"I would absolutely *love* to do that, for work, like a real career."

Felicia urged Abigail to continue designing and practicing, and when she was ready to consider different design schools, look her up. She gave the teenager her business card. "If you're looking at New York area schools, you can stay in my apartment when you interview. Email me before you apply and I'll help you put together a portfolio."

A Coffin for Callahan

On their way back to Greenville, they talked. "I guess my hunch wasn't such a hot one," said Callahan. "I was sure either your dad or Missy would have some useful information."

"Do you believe they have any useful information to give?"

"No question in your dad's case, but he's so committed to keeping his story to himself . . . I mean, if your mom's death wouldn't move him to talk, I can't imagine what would."

"So, what do we do now?"

"Let's have a nice dinner—my treat. After that, I'll catch a train or bus back to the Eastern Shore and you can take care of whatever you need to do at your mom's house. As you sort stuff out, keep your eyes open for anything that might relate to your dad's case or your mom's death. I'll be surprised if you find anything, but it never hurts to stay alert. When you come back up north on your way home to New York, we can compare notes."

"What about Monty?"

"He'll be out as soon as the investigators in the sheriff's office start using their brains. In the meantime, there's the real killer to find, and I'll focus on that."

Thirty-fourth

Carter Wingate had mixed feelings about luck. On the one hand, he considered it the last refuge of desperate people—something he never needed to rely on because he planned ahead, worked hard to execute his plan, and kept his eyes wide open to avoid being surprised by events. On the other hand, he had been the beneficiary of amazingly good luck more than once in his life, so he was forced to concede that it could be an important component of success. It had even saved his life once. Back in the nineteen-eighties, when he was a colleague of Robert Jones and lusted after the young Hazel, he had been a witness at Robert's trial, the source of bitterness that endured in Hazel Jones until her moment of death. Wingate, then known as Charlie Walton, had explained to the court that he'd seen Robert Jones at the plastics plant the night the bookkeeper was murdered. It was a shot in the dark. Jones had not been there, but since Walton had killed the bookkeeper when she discovered his embezzlement, he had to finger somebody. It was another of those rare moments when he panicked, as he had done on his boat a few nights ago when the speeding yacht appeared.

As the production manager at Dixiecraft Manufacturing, he had authority over a large budget for research and development, which allowed him to purchase expensive new equipment. His salary was adequate, but nothing special, and then as now, he was a greedy man. He also prided himself on his ability to outsmart other people. He created some shell companies, ordered fictional items from them that were never delivered, and pocketed the checks from Dixiecraft.

A Coffin for Callahan

The scam worked beautifully for about a year and half until one night when the bookkeeper found herself stranded at the plant without a ride home. Never one to waste time, the conscientious Mrs. Lambert chose to fill the dull moments while she waited for her daughter by reorganizing the purchasing files. By chance she discovered that several large pieces of equipment had been ordered and paid for, but there was no record of any of these items ever being delivered to the plant. Noticing that Charlie Walton was also working late, she asked him to help her understand the discrepancy, in effect ordering her own murder.

Smashing the small woman's skull with a foot-long iron bolt some salesman had given him years ago as a sample was easy, and it nicely eliminated the only person who knew about his embezzlement. Right away, however, Walton realized he'd traded one serious problem for another. He was the only senior manager in the plant. Although there were plenty of workers on the shop floor that night, they could (and would) provide alibis for each other. What's more, they were not permitted to be in company offices after business hours, and they had a good record of adhering to this rule. The custodial staff had already come and gone for the day, so they could not be blamed either. Walton was the only person in the building who could possibly have killed the bookkeeper. To solve that problem, he told the police—after he called them, claiming to have discovered the bookkeeper's body—that he had noticed Robert Jones, the sales manager, walking out to his car shortly before discovering the victim.

No sooner had Walton made this claim than he realized how stupid it was. Jones could be home with his family or out bowling with friends or at a church meeting, so he could have an air-tight alibi. But Lady Luck apparently had a soft spot for Charlie Walton, because Jones declined to provide an alibi. He didn't admit he was in the plant, but he didn't dispute it either. He just clammed up, citing his right against self-incrimination in response to every question he was asked, even his mailing address. He behaved this way throughout his trial, leaving the jury with no choice but to convict him. Jones appeared despondent and lost throughout the trial. His usual assertive personality seemed to have deserted him, so much so that his lawyer tried to get him off with a plea of temporary insanity, but failed. Bob must have been up to something even worse than bashing a woman's head in, thought Walton at the time, and he laughed out loud at his own unbelievable luck.

Four days is a long time when one's future is at stake, and Wingate was becoming anxious. Could luck save him again? He didn't think so. He needed to buy more time. On impulse he called the sheriff's office. He was ready to come in and make a statement implicating Monty Bergman. By revealing himself as the anonymous tipster who called earlier, he was taking a huge risk, but he would be tilting the scales his way. In the eyes of the investigators he would be cast as the conscientious neighbor, telling what he saw. At the same time he would be tightening the net around Bergman. Of course, even the dummies in Accomac would eventually realize they'd been conned, but all he needed was four days.

Thirty-fifth

Callahan found a late-night train headed north and took it. He had intended to use his time on the train to generate some new ideas about Hazel Jones's murder, but fell asleep almost as soon as he settled into his seat. The morning of the following day passed slowly and he had plenty of time to think, but his musings on the Hazel Jones case weren't productive then either. After lunch, while waiting for his bus connection in Richmond, he realized that he had no way to return home except the New York bus, which, since he could not make that connection today, would mean an overnight in Norfolk. He checked his phone and discovered that he had a number for Delbert Dix. With very little effort, he persuaded Delbert to drive more than seventy miles to pick him up. Such friendships made Callahan glad he lived on the Eastern Shore.

It wasn't until the pair had worked their way out of downtown traffic—mainly drivers mesmerized by a huge Fourth of July fireworks display at Town Point Park—that he finally had an insight. If Robert Jones was not at the plant, yet someone implicated him, that person was almost certainly the murderer of Mrs. Lambert. If Monty Bergman was not the murderer of Hazel Jones—a fact Callahan would be happy to bet his life on—yet someone implicated him also, could it be the same person in both cases? If Hazel Jones accidentally met the murderer of Mrs. Lambert, and he killed her to silence her, was he now repeating his previous action by implicating someone else? This would not be unusual. Like most people, criminals lack imagination, so they often repeat established patterns.

"You're more than usually quiet, Ed. Everything okay?"

"Fine, Delbert, fine. I've just been pondering the Hazel Jones murder some more."

"They searched that guy's house today."

"Whose house?" Callahan was still thinking of the informer, and he was astonished that the sheriff's office appeared to have done some real detective work.

"Bergman. The guy they have in jail. They went through his house top to bottom looking for clues. I saw Willie Custis at Wendy's tonight and he said when I saw you to let you know."

"Monty Bergman didn't have anything to do with the death of Hazel Jones."

"Willie said some guy had promised to come in and make a statement."

To Callahan this was good news. It suggested that the informer was getting worried that Monty might be freed and the sheriff's people would be forced to start looking for someone else. Giving a statement would keep Monty in jail and the focus of the investigation away from the informer. "Did they say who the guy was?"

"No. They're not disclosing the name, Willie said."

Callahan resolved that as soon as he got home he would talk to Willie. It was against his better judgment, because he would be encouraging Willie to do what for days he had been trying to persuade him not to do, but he needed to know the name of the person who claimed to have seen Monty on the creek that night.

They left Virginia Beach and headed out onto the trestle above the waters of the Chesapeake Bay. Traffic abruptly halted at the Thimble Shoal tunnel. Workmen were cleaning the walls of the tunnel again, which meant nighttime travelers were delayed. "So, Ed, remember how you told me that the murder stories I've been finding didn't fit with the Hazel Jones case?"

"Yep." Callahan was tired, and had been enjoying the silence.

"Well, here's one that's pretty close. See what you think. In the early nineteen-hundreds, there were two prominent doctors in Port St. George—Robards and Whalen. Dr. Robards was probably the most popular physician in the area, and Dr. Whalen was his main competition.

"On the surface, they were friendly, but nobody but they and Dr. Robards's son, also a doctor, knew that Dr. Whalen had been having an affair with Mrs. Robards."

"Doesn't sound much like the Hazel Jones case to me."

"There's definitely a resemblance. You'll see." The traffic finally began to move through the tunnel, and Delbert paused his story as he followed a police car until they were clear of the work area. "The Robards family was having a big dinner. I believe it was for Christmas, but it might have been Easter. Mrs. Robards began choking on a piece of her meal, but the father and son—both of them medical doctors, remember—stood by and did nothing. They let her choke to death, right in their family dining room."

"So where does Hazel Jones come in?"

"I'm glad you asked. Instead of calling for the police or the funeral director, they carried her body in a potato sack down to where they kept their boat on the creek. That night they took her out to some property owned by Dr. Whalen's family and dumped her there for the birds and crabs to eat."

"Didn't anybody notice she was missing?"

"Sure. But the two doctors spread the word around town that she'd had a nervous breakdown, split with her husband, and moved back to her people in Baltimore. Nobody questioned that—or maybe everyone knew about the affair already and suspected what happened and figured she deserved it."

"And her body was never found?"

"Nope. The critters did their job well."

"If I hadn't gone out on my dock to look at that fancy yacht, they might have done the same job on Mrs. Jones."

Thirty-sixth

Getting away with murdering Mrs. Lambert convinced Walton he was bullet-proof. Anyone might have had the same feeling. He experienced a kind of euphoria, believing he could do anything and get away with it. When Robert Jones was sent to prison, Walton even considered making a move on Hazel, whom he had always found very appealing, but he soon became more realistic. He had been spectacularly fortunate—once. How many times could he expect that to happen? Caution became his new watchword. A few months after the trial, he took a job with another plastics company in Ohio, and after a year moved to a third company near Seattle.

Even before he left South Carolina, he had developed a lucrative hobby of buying antiques and coins at low prices from gullible people and selling them at a large profit. He had already established a foreign bank account for his embezzlement proceeds, so it was natural to add the takings from his antique trading to the pile. He lived modestly, allowing himself certain selected, fairly inconspicuous luxuries, like fine wines and expensive shoes. He did not attempt embezzlement again, realizing that crimes in a company are almost always discovered because many people are involved. The antique and coin trading business was safer because the only two parties in each deal were the con man and his victim. What's more, many of Walton's victims were elderly, so they frequently had poor memories, which often deteriorated with time, or they sometimes died soon after selling him their valuables. As a result, most of his cheating was unlikely to be discovered by anyone.

As an added precaution, Walton eventually quit working in the plastics industry altogether, and moved to Nevada. He was becoming a rich man, so he didn't need to work at a regular job. He rented a small house in a suburb of Las Vegas popular with entertainers, bartenders, and cooks—people who worked odd hours and moved around a lot. Since he preferred to be alone most of the time, it was easy for him to remain anonymous in such a place. To complete the process, he changed his legal name to Henry Carter Wingate IV, which sounded more upscale than Charlie Walton and fit better a man born and bred in Georgia. It was a neat trick. Charlie Walton couldn't be arrested for killing the bookkeeper because Charlie Walton no longer existed, except in some dusty records in a Nevada courthouse. Carter Wingate emerged in his new role—a Southern gentleman of independent means. He changed his hair style, bought some new clothes (although in the interest of economy he kept some of his best things), and moved—first to Indiana for a few months and finally to the Eastern Shore of Virginia.

Thirty-seventh

Responding to a late night phone message, Willie Custis, Jr. was at Callahan's house first thing Tuesday morning. The young deputy, dressed in a T-shirt and shorts, was on the edge of his seat. "So does this mean you're really going to start investigating?"

"Maybe. It depends on who this informer turns out to be. I have a hunch. If I'm wrong, then there won't be any more investigating by me. Your office will need to do its own work."

"I hope you stay involved. Our people are really stuck. When I told them about the kayak not being able to carry two people, they were not happy, so they searched Monty Bergman's house to see if there was some other kind of flotation device he could have used."

"What did they find?"

"Nothing like that, but they did find a lot of stuff about Dixiecraft, which is why they're still holding him, because he has been very critical of the company where Mrs. Jones used to work and had made up a kind of charge sheet against them."

"That's bullshit."

"I sort of agree with you, but it's not my job to make those decisions. I'd like to get into investigations someday though, so I hope you'll help me learn some of the tricks you used as a detective in Philadelphia."

"It's not really about tricks, Willie. It's about never giving up until you catch somebody. But, you're forgetting. I never was a detective."

"I don't see why not. You seem to have the knack."

"Want some more coffee?"

"No, Mr. C. I'm fine."

"I like you, and I have a feeling you'll make a good officer someday, so I'm going to tell you a story. It explains why I never became a detective."

"Thanks. I appreciate your encouragement."

"This is not an encouraging story."

"That's okay."

"See if you think it's okay after you've heard it." Callahan moved the coffee cups and plates around into a neat pattern on the table. He'd never told anyone outside the police force this story before, except Doris, and he was not comfortable telling Willie, but it seemed the right thing to do.

"It was on January sixth, nineteen eighty-three. I'd been on the force for about ten years. I'd taken some courses on criminal justice and investigative techniques, had been promoted twice, and had been getting really good performance reviews. As far as I could tell, I was on track for another promotion, and then I would be able to apply to work in the detective section as a trainee investigator. That's the way they did it in those days. You were assigned to a detective squad and you went out with them on live cases and they taught you their skills on the job."

"I'd love to do that."

"And maybe you will someday. The main ingredients you need to be an investigator are a certain amount of general curiosity about things and a willingness to accept the facts you uncover—even when they don't support your pet theory."

"I could do that."

"It's not that easy, but let me go on with my story." Callahan straightened the coffee cups again. He was beginning to wish he had never started this confession, but he saw no easy way to back out. "Of course, at this time, I was still doing my regular patrol job. My partner, who was a rookie, and I were near the end of our shift. We'd been patrolling on foot through a public housing project. It was an idea somebody in the mayor's office had to make us cops seem friendlier—'neighborhood policing' they called it. It worked up to a point, especially with the older folks who had to live in those buildings and were always getting mugged or harassed in the elevators. A lot of the young ones, on the other hand, were engaged in all kinds of criminal activity, so they wished we'd stay the heck out of the projects and leave them alone.

"We came across a group of kids that looked like they might be up to some drug deals. Crack was becoming a big thing at that time, and so we always liked to bust dealers before they could get the younger kids hooked. We approached these kids and started a friendly conversation. One of the kids I knew. When he was about eleven or so he had been the catcher on a little league baseball team I coached for a while. I hadn't seen him in at least five years, and I should have realized how much a boy could change in that time.

"Instead, I let down my guard. We asked them what they were doing. We didn't get truthful answers, but that was typical. One of the other kids had a vest with pockets bulging with something, and I asked if they minded if I took a look at the vest. The kid didn't say yes or no, so I started to reach for it. Another kid—the one I knew—pulled a small semi-automatic pistol out of his jacket and pointed it at my partner. He said, 'You cops back off or I shoot.'"

A Coffin for Callahan

"He was looking at my partner, not at me, and I could easily have decked him or gone for my weapon, which probably would have made him point the pistol at me. Instead, I hesitated. I tried to talk to him, as I had before when we were playing baseball together. It was the stupidest fucking thing I've ever done in my life.

"He didn't answer me. He just smiled a strange kind of smile and pulled the trigger, hitting my partner square in the face. At that point I charged, knocking him down, but he still held the pistol, so I held his arm down—he was much smaller than me—pulled out my weapon and shot him in the middle of his chest. He died in less than a minute. Naturally, the other kids ran for cover.

"When I turned to my partner, he was lying on the pavement in a huge pool of blood. I couldn't believe anybody could bleed that much and not be dead. The EMTs took him to the hospital, and he was in a coma for thirteen days before he finally died. I got a reprimand and demotion—not for letting my partner get killed—but for using excessive force shooting and killing the kid. I don't think they cared jack shit about what I did to that kid, but they wanted to punish me somehow for not protecting a fellow officer. That was the real end of my police career. Because of the union, they couldn't kick me out, but I was assigned to routine patrols and various desk duties nobody else liked to do until I reached twenty years and qualified for early retirement. Then they told me: 'If you try to stay on longer, we'll find a way to fire you,' so I took retirement."

"Gosh, Mr. C., that's a horrible story."

"About as horrible as they come, but at least it explains why I never made detective and I'm retired on the Eastern Shore."

A Coffin for Callahan

$* * *$

Willie wasn't to go on duty until three in the afternoon, and even then there was no guarantee he would be able to get the name of the informer. Callahan decided he might as well try to keep busy until he had some news. He had been away from his coffin and bluebirds too long. First, he went to see the bluebirds. When he saw no birds anywhere, he checked the nest, which was empty. While he was away over the weekend, the babies must have fledged, and the whole family departed for heaven knows where. It bothered him that he didn't know how many baby birds there had been. He hoped they were all right. He took a moment and prayed that they were all right. Then he opened the bottom of the box and pushed the old nest out. Some other species might choose to use it later in the summer. If they didn't, in the fall he would take it into his shop and scrub it out with soap and hot water to prepare it for another season.

Next, he went to look over the coffin. It was basically complete, although it still had no handles. As heavy as it was, it would definitely need them. He planned to add two extra handles not specified in the plans because his coffin was slightly larger and a lot heavier than a pine coffin. He also intended to make the rope handles out of five-quarter inch line, which was larger than the plans called for or was needed for strength, but seemed like it would be more comfortable for the hands of the pallbearers. The first step was to mark and then drill twenty holes of one and five-sixteenths inches diameter around the periphery of the coffin, three inches below the edge—two on the head, two on the foot, and eight on each side. He made a

165

little jig for marking, and that task passed quickly. He was especially pleased with himself that he remembered to back drill each hole after he was part way through so there was no splitting of the wood.

The line he had chosen for handles was dark blue—a good cop color he thought—five-quarter, double-braided nylon line dock line. It was soft and supple and would feel good on the hands of those who would carry him to his final resting place. He'd paid nearly two hundred and fifty dollars for only twenty-five feet. Ten dollars a foot was more than he'd ever paid for any rope or much of anything else before, but because dying was a once-in-lifetime experience, he felt like indulging himself. He had handle material with a breaking strength of eighteen tons—suitable to restrain a boat up to one hundred and fifty feet long according to the manufacturer's catalog. Superfluous, of course, for coffin handles, but it gave exactly the look he wanted.

Callahan knotted one end of the line and put the other end out through a hole in one corner and threaded it back in and out again through all of the holes, ending at the hole adjacent to the one where he started. Then he went around the coffin, adjusting the amount of line for each handle. He wanted the handles to be fairly close to the coffin sides for appearance sake, but far enough away so nobody would have trouble getting his fingers behind the handle. When satisfied, he marked the cutoff point and pulled the end of the line out. He cut carefully with a razor blade and then whipped the cut end as near as he could to the way the factory had done the other end.

With the line in place, and knotted at both ends, as many as ten people could be pallbearers and each of them would have an excellent grip so there would be no embarrassing dropping of the coffin—unless, being so close together, they tripped over each other's feet and all fell down in a heap. Callahan smiled at the prospect that ten people could be found among his acquaintances and friends who would be both willing and able to carry his earthly remains. He cleaned up the shop and then went in the house to mix up a cold iced tea.

Thirty-eighth

On his way back from making his signed statement, Wingate began to feel nostalgic about the Eastern Shore. He'd had a good life there, and was sorry it was ending. As he drove, he recalled one of his earlier, very satisfying local experiences. He often replayed such experiences in his mind with great pleasure. In this case, the vanquished client had been a retired doctor who lived only a few miles away. In an effort to maintain his low profile, Wingate rarely did business on the Shore, but had heard that the doctor's wife died and the man was eager to clear out his house full of antiques so he could move closer to his grandchildren. The opportunity for a quick profit proved irresistible.

Wingate presented himself at the elderly physician's house, and very quickly determined that there was little of significant value except a very old portrait of a country gentleman and his wife. The doctor couldn't remember where the painting came from, but thought his late wife bought it as an investment decades ago. He'd never liked the painting, and thought his wife had wasted her money, and he couldn't remember how much she paid, who the artist was, or anything else about it.

Wingate took the painting off the wall and noticed a sales slip attached to the back with yellowing cellophane tape: *JJ Audubon 1821, $5000.* Deftly pocketing the piece of paper, he claimed to the gullible physician that his observation of the back of the painting showed there was damage that would eventually develop into a crack visible on the front, Wingate offered the doctor twenty-five hundred dollars, saying it would cost him a thousand to have the defect corrected. The old man gladly accepted his check, but not half as gladly as Wingate accepted a payment of one hundred and eighty thousand from an auction house a year later. This triumph was one of his fondest memories, and it reinforced his view of himself as a man who knew how to turn any situation to his advantage.

His experience with the doctor also reinforced a conviction of his based on years of cheating people: honest people make the best suckers. People who would never cheat someone else assume that most other people don't cheat either, which makes them fatted calves, ready for the slaughter. On the other hand, whenever Wingate felt someone was trying to scam *him*, he always broke off dealing and retreated. He didn't want a battle of wits with another con man. The key to his winning was not his skill at spinning a good story, although that was essential. The key was picking the right victims.

Upon returning home, Wingate treated himself to a glass of wine and decided to take it easy and read the paper. He had done most of his preparations for leaving the country, and his signed statement to the bumbling county officials incriminating his young neighbor should buy him the three days he needed. Under the headline WHEN DEATH STALKED THE SHORE, he read about a young historian named Dix who was researching Eastern Shore murders and their perpetrators for a book he was planning to call *Historic Murders of the Eastern Shore*. As an example of the stories Dix was uncovering, the paper mentioned a 1926 case in Daugherty in which a young woman's fiancé stabbed his future mother-in-law to death at a pre-wedding party. She had never liked the young man. Since he received forty years in the penitentiary and the wedding never happened, in death she had her revenge. Another case, from

A Coffin for Callahan

July 7, 1887, on Chincoteague, involved an oysterman named William Draper who stabbed a Captain Theodore Lloyd over a petty dispute. Lloyd was expected to die immediately, but slowly recovered. Draper was arrested right after the incident, but broke out of jail and left "for parts unknown," as the newspaper put it. Later in the summer, Lloyd became seriously ill, presumably from injuries sustained when he was stabbed. He was sent to Philadelphia for treatment, but died when the doctors admitted there was nothing they could do to save him. Wingate noted with amusement how the date of the stabbing, July seventh, and his own chosen date to leave the Shore "for parts unknown" were the same. He smiled. He had that lucky feeling again. He did not intend to ever be mentioned in Mr. Dix's book.

Thirty-ninth

No sooner had Callahan sat down at the kitchen table with Saturday's paper than there was a tapping on his screen door. "Yoo hoo! Edward!"

"I'm in the kitchen, Eileen." He didn't get up.

By now Mrs. Davis had made her way to the kitchen, a plate of sugar cookies in the shape of stars in her hand. Each cookie was decorated with red white and blue sprinkles. "I made these for you to celebrate the Fourth, but you weren't home yet, so I'm bringing them over now."

"Thank you." The look on her face suggested that Mrs. Davis expected some information in return for the cookies, so he said, "Felicia and I were still in South Carolina after visiting her father in prison."

"How nice, bringing the family together in a time of tragedy."

"It wasn't that nice. He refused to talk."

"I'm sorry. But, of course, you had to try. Nothing ventured, nothing gained."

"We also talked to the daughter of the woman he supposedly killed."

"You're very persistent. Willie says that's a good trait for an investigator."

"True, but we didn't get anything from her either." Callahan took one of the cookies and tried it. "These are good. Thanks. My coffin is basically finished. Want to see it?"

"You know how I feel about that project of yours, Edward, but if it will please you to show me . . . ."

A Coffin for Callahan

They went to the workshop and Callahan showed off the coffin and the line he'd prepared for the handles. Much to Mrs. Davis's dismay, he climbed in and lay down inside the box. "See! It's a perfect fit."

"Edward, please. You know how much it hurts me to imagine you going the way of my dear Preston Lee. Do remove yourself from that thing, now."

Sitting up in the coffin, he said, "This afternoon I plan to do a rough sanding all over and a first coat of finish. In the next few days I'll do a couple more coats and it'll be ready for prime time."

"Please, Edward."

He stood up in the coffin and then hopped out, landing lightly on the floor. "Don't worry. I don't intend to use it anytime soon."

"I *do* worry. You should take better care of yourself. I'm going home."

Callahan felt a little guilty as he watched Mrs. Davis walk away, but at the same time pleased that he'd finally discovered a way to make her leave.

With Mrs. Davis gone, he decided he might as well start sanding, but then remembered that he had neglected to put guides on the coffin lid. He quickly cut these from a thin scrap and installed them with small nails and glue. He should have waited for the glue to set completely, but he was eager to see what a coat of finish would look like. He sanded the bottom of the coffin first, then the sides, and finally the lid, taking care not to be too rough on the newly installed guides. Then he cleaned the dust from all the surfaces with his vacuum turned up to its maximum power level, and followed this with a careful wipe-down with a soft terry cloth, turning it often as he went.

As he had hoped, applying a mixture of lacquer and tung oil—an idea from a friend who read about it on the Internet—to the smooth, clean wood surface produced a deepening of the grain pattern and color. The dark blue parts of the grain resembled deep, mysterious canyons and the light parts looked like golden ridges in the terrain of a distant planet. He was going to have one very exotic coffin, and he loved it.

With his finishing done, Callahan closed the doors of his workshop—very carefully, to avoid stirring up dust, and then he did something unusual. He sat on his back porch and drank a couple of beers alone. He felt like celebrating, even if he had nobody to celebrate with. His coffin was looking much better than he had ever expected it would when he began the project. He wished Doris could to see it. She would have been proud and delighted to share his success. And, unlike Mrs. Davis, she would have understood his need to build the thing. Of course, if she were alive, he would have built new kitchen cabinets instead, but now was a time for savoring the moment, not for logical thinking. While pondering whether to continue his celebration with a dinner out, he heard a familiar tap-tap-tap on his front door. Reluctantly, he strolled through the house.

Mrs. Davis, frowning in a way he'd rarely seen, said, "Willie called a few minutes ago and asked me to tell you something."

"Come in, Eileen." Mrs. Davis was not the woman he was thinking about, and he was not very happy to see her.

"He's worried, but he didn't want to contact you directly."

"About what?"

A Coffin for Callahan

"That Bergman boy. A witness came to the sheriff's office and gave a statement. He told them he saw Monty Bergman take something out into the creek and dump it the night Mrs. Jones died."

"I don't believe it."

"Well, that's what the person said."

"Who?"

"Willie didn't say."

"Then I want to talk to Willie."

"That would not be a good idea, because he's been criticized by his boss for talking to you. They say you're interfering with the investigation."

"I'm only interfering with their determination to make fools of themselves! Monty didn't do it, and it's likely their witness is the real killer. Tell Willie that."

"Oh, Lordy! Do you really think so? I'll call him right now."

As Mrs. Davis disappeared across the street, Callahan decided he'd better stay close to home. He'd made a provocative statement about the witness to induce Willie to contact him, and he felt a little embarrassed by his shady tactics.

Callahan made a couple of tuna fish salad sandwiches, which he washed down with a third beer, followed by a cup of black coffee. He didn't enjoy his dinner much, but he had been hungry before, and now he wasn't, so the meal had done its job. Normally an evening stroll to see how the bluebirds were doing would be his next move, to deliver a pleasing emotional boost before he settled in for the night. But there were no bluebirds to see anymore, and even the fabulous orange sun settling into the trees along St. George Creek did nothing for his troubled spirit. He couldn't put his finger on the source of his disquiet. He sat on his bench, slapping the occasional mosquito, but more often slapping himself where a mosquito had been.

He had never liked waiting. A great deal of police work required one to wait and wait, and then wait some more. Parades didn't start on time, court proceedings ran beyond their prescribed time limits, celebrities' limos were late from the airport, and many stakeouts never produced any results. Now he was waiting for Willie Custis to call when he would rather be taking some action, but without more information, there was no action worth taking. Monty had been arrested on what Callahan was sure was no credible evidence. Even after only a few days of knowing her, he adored Felicia like the daughter he never had, and the idea that she should be suffering because her boyfriend was in jail made Callahan very angry. Another mosquito bit him, and he slapped himself hard on the ear. It seemed to jolt his mind in precisely the right way, and he knew what he needed to do. To hell with the sheriff's office, he thought. He headed back to the house to call Willie.

As it happened, the call was not needed. When he picked up the phone, he discovered a phone message—very cryptic and conspiratorial—from Mrs. Davis. "You will be having a visitation, from the one you were asking about, after eleven o'clock tonight. Be patient, Edward. Good things come to him who waits."

Mrs. Davis's message sounded like a religious prophecy, and Callahan could not help but laugh. He tried watching TV, but fell asleep. At around eleven-thirty he was awakened by a gentle rapping on his screen door. "Mr. C. It's me, Willie."

Still slightly in a daze, he opened the door. "How're you doing, Willie? Thanks for coming."

"I'm fine, but I can't stay long, and I really shouldn't be here."

"It's a free country."

"I know, but my supervisor is becoming really annoyed with me for getting advice from you. I still believe you know better than any of them what's going on, but they don't like me talking to you. They're saying I should be sticking to my patrol duties and not investigating."

"They're absolutely right. From now on, I'll do all the investigating, but to do that I need to know a couple of things. Tell me, first, what exactly did this guy say?"

"Of course, I haven't read his statement, but what I've been told is that he said Monty Bergman was able to float the body because he put it on a tow tube that he pulled with his kayak."

"Come on! Monty doesn't have a motor boat. Why in Christ's name would he spend four hundred bucks on a tow tube? Did they find this tow tube?

"No. And it does seem strange that he would have one if he doesn't own a towboat, now that you mention it, but that's what the guy said."

"What guy? What's his name?"

"I really shouldn't say."

"Yes, you should. Monty Bergman did not kill Mrs. Jones. Your witness is a liar. I want to know who the hell he is."

"Promise you won't say who told you."

"I promise, Willie, that nobody will ever know where I got the information."

"Okay. I'm actually glad to tell you, because I don't think Monty Bergman seems like the murderer type. You're more likely to find the real killer than our guys."

"We'll see. What do you have?"

"The man who came to us appears to be very respectable. He's Monty's next-door neighbor."

"Name?"

"Carter Wingate. I made the connection when I saw this guy in our office with the letters CW monogrammed on his shirt pocket. I happened to pass him in the hallway when he came in, before I'd heard his name. I thought it was some kind of new shirt brand and I was trying to figure out what it stood for."

"You're observant."

"I'm trying to sharpen my skills every chance I get, so I look for details on people. Later I found out his name was Henry Carter Wingate, but he doesn't usually use Henry. He calls himself Carter."

"So what did he say?"

"As I said, I never read the statement, but I talked for a while with the girl who transcribed it from the tape. She said he saw Monty Bergman go out late on the night of the murder towing the tube behind his kayak. There was something in a plastic bag tied onto the tube with yellow rope."

"Very colorful, but they never found this tube right?"

"Right, but the witness, Mr. Wingate, said he saw Monty come back an hour later without it—only with the kayak."

"Why did Wingate sit up until the middle of the night?"

"The girl didn't say."

"Did the shirt look old?"

"What shirt?"

"The one with the CW monogram. Did that shirt look old to you?"

"It was a plain white, button-down dress shirt, with nothing special about it that I noticed."

Callahan felt like celebrating. "Want a beer?"

"I'd better be going. They've rotated me to morning shift for tomorrow, so I have to be up at six."

"Thanks, Willie, I'll keep you up to date through your aunt, okay?"

"That's the best way. Goodnight, Mr. C."

Fortieth

Time was running out for Wingate, who had many details to attend to before his Thursday departure. Prioritizing, he decided to first rid himself of the metal items that had belonged to Hazel Jones. He would have liked to keep them as mementos, but in matters such as avoiding arrest, his self-protective instincts always trumped his emotions. He had a small plastic bag of keys, a zipper, a couple of brass buttons, two rings, a lipstick case, and a pocket calculator. His initial idea had been to take a short boat ride and lose the items in the creek near the dredged channel where props of passing boats would quickly entomb them in mud. However, he was feeling slightly lazy, and was beginning to worry that taking the boat out might look suspicious, although he was fairly confident nobody would be watching. Besides, he was feeling lucky again. Trash collection was the next day. He wrapped the small collection of incriminating objects in a crumpled ball of paper he used to wrap the fish he had grilled for dinner the previous night. He put the paper ball inside a small trash bag with some other unwanted stuff and tossed it into his bin.

Next he called a local moving company to confirm that his household goods would be packed and moved to Texas, where he had arranged for storage in a public warehouse. At some future date, probably acting through a lawyer he would hire in Central America, the goods could be shipped out of the country to another warehouse, perhaps in Mexico. Eventually he would get all his treasures back again, although it would take a while. The moving men were to arrive next Monday, after Wingate would be safely out of the country, but probably before the sheriff's office had begun to wonder about him. Expecting them to be slow at figuring things out, he felt confident that when they finally came looking they would find an empty house and nobody at home to answer their questions.

Next he gave his car a good vacuuming and rinsed the dust off with a garden hose. Worrying that his efforts were insufficient to thwart even the most inept forensic expert, he made a mental note to get the car detailed before he left. He'd also arranged to have the lawn mowed for two weeks and to have his mail held for two weeks. This was the length of his usual vacation, and he congratulated himself on how clever he had been to leave evidence suggesting he would be coming back.

Forty-first

"Mr. Callahan?"

"Hi, Felicia, I'm sorry to call so late."

"What's wrong?"

"Nothing, but I need some information. How old was the guy Charlie Walton that you mentioned—the witness who claimed he saw your dad the night of Mrs. Lambert's murder?"

"I don't know exactly. I was a kid at the time, and I don't remember what he looked like if I ever saw him. Maybe I never did."

"Would he have been more or less the age of your parents?"

"Probably not much older. Actually, I really don't know."

"You said he moved away. Do you know where he went?"

"No. I wish I could be more helpful."

"Don't worry about it. But if you find anything about him in your mom's things, save it for me, okay?"

Callahan was feeling good. He opened another beer. In many ways, he'd never felt right since moving to the Shore—until now. How odd, he thought, that now, of all times, I'm feeling almost giddy with joy, as if I'd won the lottery. Could it really be that finishing my coffin was the cause? Could it be the beer? It was neither, and he knew it. He was the anticipating the hunt. He was going to find out if Carter Wingate was Charlie Walton. Whoever he was, Callahan would find the evidence to put him away. He would avenge Hazel Jones the best way he knew, by doing the job he'd spent his life preparing for.

* * *

A Coffin for Callahan

At 5 a.m. Callahan's alarm went off, but he had been awake for several minutes. Despite having barely four and half hours' sleep, he felt energized. Today would be fun. He had a quick cup of coffee and some toast with jam, and then grabbed the items he would need—bottled water, a hat, Doris's birding telescope, and her camera with its zoom lens. He barely knew how to operate the camera, but assumed he would figure it out if the need arose. Soon he was motoring down St. George Creek. He kept the outboard at a low speed until he was clear of the No-Wake zone near the town wharf, mainly to avoid disturbing the neighbors and visiting yachtsmen asleep on their boats. Then he gunned it.

Despite its small motor, in a short time his little boat had brought him opposite Finley's Bar. The sun was beginning to make its way above the horizon, pouring brilliant golden light over a row of houses on the south side of the creek. Disturbed from its roost on a daymark by the early morning navigator, an osprey circled warily around the boat. It was only then that Callahan realized the flaw in his plan. He didn't know which house he should be looking at. There were several houses of various sizes and styles in the row, and all he knew was that Carter Wingate lived in one of them and was Monty's next-door neighbor. From what Felicia had said, he knew that Monty's house was small and had solar panels on it. He scanned the creek edge with the telescope looking for Monty's place. Shortly he noticed a very small, new looking house partially obscured by pine trees. He couldn't see any solar panels, but realized that when viewed from the north they would be hidden on the opposite side of the house. Adjacent to the possible Monty Bergman house was a large house surrounded by pink and blue hydrangeas, with an extensive lawn and carefully tended garden. The house looked very old, but with a couple of modern additions that lent it a sprawling appearance. For lack of any other good candidates, he concluded this was the house he was looking for. Now what?

It was still very early in the morning, so it seemed unlikely that anyone would be up and about. He tried using a checklist approach. The location was right, based on where the concrete block anchor was found. It was also a perfect place for viewing Monty Bergman's comings and goings. To be a credible witness, the man would need convince the sheriff's people that he could actually see Monty leaving his property in a kayak, and that was definitely possible from this house, although almost as easy from any of the other houses along the row. The house had a dock and a boat. In fact, the immaculate Boston Whaler that Callahan observed there looked like a much better conveyance for a body than Monty's kayak with a tube in tow. Had there been no boat and no dock, Callahan probably would have been inclined to let Carter Wingate off the hook, but they were there, so he was still fair game.

Suddenly, a little white dog burst out the back door of the house and ran across the lawn, apparently chasing a squirrel. He was followed by a middle-aged man wearing a bathrobe and white rubber boots. Callahan put down the telescope and grabbed Doris's camera. It was only then that he noticed how many controls it had. Various switches and dials were marked by incredibly small, cryptic icons that he could barely see and had no hope of understanding without the manual, which he'd left at home in the camera case. He moved all the dials to "Auto," reasoning that that would be the most foolproof. Then he started looking for an "On" switch. In the meantime, the man seemed happy to throw sticks for the dog and wander about the lawn. Callahan prayed, which he rarely did, but had been doing more often lately, that the man would stay outside until he got the camera figured out.

He pushed a button marked "Zoom" and the lens extended itself until it was nearly a foot and a half long. Apparently the camera had been turned on ever since he chose "Auto," or maybe it was always on, waiting for someone to touch it to wake it up. He looked through the viewfinder and saw blades of grass as big as cornstalks filling the whole frame. Desperately he tried to find the man, but everything was enlarged so much he only saw individual leaves, the water, hydrangea blooms as big as basketballs, gargantuan boulders on the shore, and the man's huge right foot—before it moved. Callahan tried pushing "Zoom" again and the lens retracted. This time he could see the whole scene and the man looked like a bug. He tried pushing "Zoom" while looking and pointing at the man's face.

Amazingly, when the face filled nearly the whole frame, the man was looking straight at Callahan across the water. It was like a mug shot, but much better quality than most of them. Callahan pushed what he assumed was the correct button and heard a click. He looked up, but the man and dog had disappeared. Not knowing whether he had a picture or not, but confident from the way the man retreated so quickly from the camera that this must be Carter Wingate, Callahan started the engine and turned his boat toward home.

Forty-second

Wednesday did not start well. When releasing Orion for his usual early morning rip and tear around the yard, Wingate looked out at St. George Creek and saw a man in a boat. He had a camera with a huge zoom lens, which was pointed straight at him. He turned and dashed inside as quickly as he could, but could not help wondering whether he had been quick enough. Except for his driver's license and passport, there were no recent photos of him anywhere, and he intended to keep it that way.

Breakfast did little to relieve his anxiety. Who was this man, and what was he doing taking pictures of me? Wingate didn't like it at all. However, he had a good plan, he knew it was a good plan, and it was going well. All he had to do was remain calm and follow the plan. By noon tomorrow he would be on his way to the airport.

In the meantime, a couple of guys were to come at nine o'clock and detail his car. It seemed an odd thing to do—have your car meticulously cleaned before leaving the country for good—but the aim was to rid the vehicle of as much of Hazel Jones as possible. He was sure these people could do a more thorough job then he could, and having his car cleaned added further evidence suggesting he planned to return.

As he waited for the detailers, he began to fret about the grandfather clock. Damn! It had been a delicious victory, but how these local movers, whose main experience was shuffling around cheap furniture belonging to poor people, would ever pack such a delicate and valuable antique was beyond him. Regardless, he had given their boss detailed written instructions, and he was going to have to trust them. The clock was one of his prize pieces, not just because he loved it, but because he acquired in the classic Carter Wingate manner. Just recalling his big win made him feel better.

Although it had been an easy walk from his B&B on Cape May's New York Avenue to the antique shop, Wingate drove. When he parked in front of Time Was on the nearly deserted Ocean Street, the door was locked and there was a Closed sign in the window. He had the elderly owner's home phone number, so he called immediately. "Myron, where the hell are you?" he scolded.

"I'm having a small reaction to my medication, Mr. Wingate. I'll be there soon."

"Don't take all day."

Wingate's approach to dealers was very different from the way he handled amateurs. Amateurs were to be flattered, seduced, or befriended, to make them believe he was on their side and cared about their welfare. Once the victim's trust had been acquired, it was easy to steer him or (usually) her wherever he wanted. With dealers, who normally knew the value of the goods being traded, the idea was to dominate. He had to show them he was the boss, abuse them until they felt helpless and beaten, so when he made his final offer, they yielded in a feeble attempt to preserve a particle of dignity. The beauty of Wingate's approach was that, upon discovering how easily they had been bullied out of a valuable piece of merchandise, most dealers—to avoid embarrassment—never told anyone. They covered Wingate's tracks for him, keeping others in the trade from finding out what a scoundrel he was.

Wingate moved his car down the block. The old man's tardiness in opening his shop was a gift. By being late, the dealer had already conceded a psychological advantage. When he arrived at his shop to find Wingate gone, he would fear that he had lost the opportunity to trade, giving even more advantage to Wingate. After an appropriate delay to let the man become disgusted with himself and desperate, Wingate would appear in front of the shop—a vulture pretending to be a dove.

After ten minutes or so, a rust stained Buick station wagon stopped in front of the shop. Watching in his rear-view mirror, Wingate gloated. The clunky old car was further evidence of the old man's financial vulnerability. The dealer got out, awkwardly pulling a cane off the back seat. Slowly he crossed the sidewalk and entered his shop. Wingate waited five minutes, then drove around the block and stopped behind the Buick. He knocked loudly on the shop door.

Forty-third

As he motored at half throttle toward his dock, Callahan used his time on placid St. George Creek to think. If he had captured a good picture of Carter Wingate, he had something to compare with Charlie Walton's photo if he could ever obtain one. Perhaps Felicia would find a picture in an old company Christmas party photo or a newspaper clipping from the time of her father's trial. Or, he could try to find Charlie Walton on the Internet. The latter approach would be a problem, because he would have to ask Mrs. Davis for help again, incurring a debt he would be expected to repay.

Recalling Doris conjured memories of his own youth and how much the beginning of Monty and Felicia's relationship resembled his start with Doris. Maybe that was why he felt so attached to the young couple despite barely knowing either of them. His relationship with Doris had begun as a chance encounter that led almost immediately to a love lasting a lifetime.

Only three weeks out of the Police Academy, he had been assigned to foot patrol in a neighborhood along the Delaware River a couple of miles south of his home. That year was the last one in which Philadelphia used routine foot patrols, and all the cops knew they would be getting shiny new cars soon and putting away their heavy shoes. Patrolling on foot was passé, and the men who did motor patrols were already beginning to look down their noses at anybody who still walked the neighborhoods.

For Callahan, being a new officer was such a thrill that he didn't pay any attention to the rapidly diminishing prestige of his assignment. He checked doors, helped people cross the street, blocked traffic so neighbors could parallel park their cars in the narrow streets, and generally made himself useful. After only three evenings of work, he was becoming a well-known figure in the neighborhood. All the kids knew Officer Callahan, and when he told them he thought it might be getting close to their bedtimes, they went home without protest, feeling honored that this representative of the City of Brotherly Love, with his shiny new badge, had spoken to each of them by name.

One evening he came upon a young woman and an elderly lady with a flimsy two-wheeled utility cart bursting with groceries. The two women were down on their knees on the sidewalk, trying to figure out how to put a broken wheel back on. He offered to help, but realized right away that the wheel was so badly bent that even if he could force it onto the axle, it would not turn. "Do you have far to go?" he asked.

"To the end of this block," said the young woman.

In that moment, looking in her dark brown eyes, he realized he was in love. He'd never been in love before, and indeed never thought much about settling down, believing it would be wise to establish his police career before becoming serious with anyone. Too late. The young woman was Doris. By the time they reached her house—with him carrying the cart full of groceries while the two women protested all the way they didn't really need his help—he knew her name, her mother's name, and her phone number. The pair went to the movies the first evening he was off duty, and were married on the one-year anniversary of the day they met.

But that was all in the past, and in the present it was not yet 7 a.m.—too early for calling Felicia, and definitely too early for asking a favor of Mrs. Davis. He tied up his boat, went in and warmed up a cup of leftover coffee and headed for his workshop. In the hour or so he had free he could do a light sand of the coffin and maybe apply a second coat of finish. As he sanded, he planned his next move. First, find out if Carter Wingate was Charlie Walton. If not, he had no plan after that. There was no evidence at all of Carter Wingate's involvement in Hazel Jones's murder, no matter how plausible that scenario seemed to Callahan. If the Wingate and Walton were indeed the same man, he had no plan for that either, but he knew he would need to tread carefully to avoid giving his quarry a second chance to run.

He completed the sanding and carefully wiped off the coffin and lid with a clean towel, turning it often. Then, taking great care to work slowly to avoid stirring up dust, he methodically applied the second coat of his lacquer and tung oil mixture, trying to remember to brush only in one direction. The pure joy of watching the beautiful wood open up before his eyes was almost enough to distract him from what he must do later that morning.

* * *

When he called, Felicia said, "I'm nearly finished sorting the house, and should be coming north in a day or two."

"Did you find anything related to your dad's trial—like a picture of Charlie Walton?"

"Surprisingly, no. The way Mom used to talk about it, and as angry as she was about Charlie Walton, I assumed it was very important to her, but she seems to have saved nothing."

"Sorry to hear it," Callahan replied. "Have a safe trip up."

A Coffin for Callahan

Having failed with Felicia, Callahan went to call on Mrs. Davis. He had gone to Mrs. Davis's house alone only once before—the morning after Doris died. Mrs. Davis came to his house often enough, so he hardly needed to visit her. He didn't want to do anything to encourage more visits, but this time he needed her assistance.

"Good morning, Eileen," he said.

"Why, Edward, what a delightful surprise!" She smoothed her hair and smiled. "Good things come to him—or her—who waits. Do come in."

After some more coffee, freshly baked biscuits with jam, and much fluttering, Callahan asked Mrs. Davis to come over to his house and help him use Doris's computer to try to find Charlie Walton. She was clearly disappointed that he was focused on his objective and not on socializing with her, but assisted him anyway. The first search on a people-finder web site yielded ninety-seven Charlie Waltons, of whom about a dozen were dead and the rest did not appear to be anywhere near old enough. Another web site revealed more than two hundred Charlie Waltons. Callahan even paid several dollars each to look at the data for a few of the most promising ones in terms of residence address and age, but none were even close in appearance to the man he had seen on the lawn, even allowing for age, clothing, and hair style.

"Why do you care about this Walton fellow anyway?"

He had been hoping that question would not be asked, because he didn't want the story to get back to nephew Willie, at least not yet, so he did something he almost never did. He lied. "He's an old classmate of mine from the high school. When I was out on my boat this morning I thought of him—hadn't had his name in my head in years—but after that, I couldn't shake him, so I thought, why not look him up?"

"You made a very good try. And as I often tell people, 'Nothing ventured, nothing gained.' Give me just a moment and I'll run home and get you a couple more biscuits for later."

While Mrs. Davis was out of the room, Callahan tried one last idea. He typed in "Carter Wingate." He tried three different sites. On two of them, no such person was found. The third site had three Carter Wingates, of whom two were under thirty years old, and the third was in Wyoming. None of them lived on the Eastern Shore of Virginia or had ever lived there. To Callahan, this negative result was actually a positive. It showed clearly that the man he had photographed that morning was determined to leave no trace, which was to be expected if his real name were Charlie Walton.

After once again praising Mrs. Davis's biscuits, Callahan was rewarded with an explanation of how to get photos off Doris's camera and print them. He printed several very nice bird pictures he never knew his wife had taken, and waited until Mrs. Davis had gone home to prepare for a garden club meeting before he printed the one he really wanted. Carter Wingate stared at him with the look of a panicked deer. The fit with Callahan's expectation was too good. He was beginning to fear his objectivity was failing him.

Despite his lack of any need for more coffee and sweets, Callahan headed for the bakery. He'd spent too much time at the computer, and the desire to stroll somewhere—anywhere—was great. That late in the morning the place was nearly deserted, but Delbert Dix was there. "Good morning, Ed, how are things?"

Callahan didn't want to share his suspicions with anyone local, so he began by reviewing his progress on the coffin instead. This did not interest Delbert.

"So you're not looking into Hazel Jones's murder anymore?"

"I was never looking into her murder really, only sharing some ideas once in a while."

"Too bad, because Willie told me they don't have a lot to go on with this Monty Bergman guy. Looks like another blind alley. He's beginning to worry they'll never find anybody, which has happened in several of the murders I've been researching. For example, yesterday I was reading about another woman who was strangled, and they never found her killer either."

"Recently?"

"Compared to some of the other murders I've read about, yes. It was in 1964. This lady, Minerva Dean, was a widow who worked in a market on Chincoteague. One day she didn't show up for work. When somebody went to look for her, they found her half naked in her own bed, with one of her stockings tied around her neck, which was kind of weird, because the coroner decided she had been strangled by hand and then the stocking was tied on later, long after she died."

"And they found nobody they could pin it on?"

"Right. They interviewed a couple of guys, but decided they weren't the one. They then sent a bunch of fingerprints to the FBI and brought in the state police to help them. They also interviewed somebody in Delaware, but again with no result. Ultimately, they gave up."

A Coffin for Callahan

After leaving the bakery, Callahan walked home slowly. The thought of nobody ever being found and prosecuted for killing a person was deeply troubling. He had a clear sense of right and wrong, and somebody getting away with murder was about as wrong as anything could be in his book.

The phone rang. "It was only one thin folder," Felicia said. "It was sandwiched in with lots of boring stuff like income tax forms and electric bills. There are three newspaper clippings about the trial, and one of them shows pictures of my dad and Charlie Walton."

"Can you send it?"

"What if I bring it with me tomorrow?"

"I'd like it now."

"I could scan it and send it in an email."

"I'm not sure I'd know how to open it, and I don't want Mrs. Davis to know about this 'cause she'll blab to Willie. Can you fax it?" Callahan gave her the number of the local print shop where he knew he could retrieve a fax. "Please call me the minute you send it."

Forty-fourth

"Good morning, Mr. Wingate," said the dealer. "I am truly sorry to have kept you waiting." His right hand trembled miserably as he offered a limp handshake.

Wingate pressed. "We must not dilly-dally. I had to call one of my clients and ask her to change our appointment." Lying about a non-existent customer was a way to further burden the old man about his tardiness. Making it clear that they had little time to act further tilted the playing field in Wingate's favor. He'd honed these techniques over the years to the point that they came naturally, without thought.

"From your email, I understand that we have a tentative deal," said the dealer. "May I see the pearls, please?"

"I would like to look at the clock again first. I want to make sure it's as I remember it." This additional demand was more jockeying for advantage, and it worked.

"It's right at the back of the shop, near the armoire. I cleaned it and wound it myself yesterday. You'll see it keeps nearly perfect time."

Wingate went to look at the clock. He dawdled, even though he could see immediately that the long case clock was in mint condition and was only about a minute fast compared to his vintage Breitling. In the reflection of the clock face, he could see the old man watching him intently, hungrily. "It will do," he said when he returned to the jewelry counter where the old man had seated himself on a rickety stool. Slowly Wingate reached in his pocket and pulled out a battered jewelry case—no sense in giving away a good one, he thought the day before when he transferred the pearls from the Tiffany case they came in to this one. He opened the case and pushed it across the counter.

The elderly dealer examined each of the three strands carefully by eye and with a loupe. He hefted each strand and held it up to the light. He then pulled out a portable black light from inside his counter and turned it on. He smiled a wan smile. "These are excellent, Mr. Wingate, although somewhat worn."

"They're antiques."

"Of course, but we always hope to find a string that was not used too much."

"You just said they were excellent."

"Excellent for what they are is what I meant to say. The one of with the gold clasp—about 1880 vintage perhaps—is probably worth more than the other two combined."

"No need to wrap the clock for me. I brought my own pads."

"What I am trying to say, Mr. Wingate, is that the clock is a Frances Paxton from 1778. It's worth more than fifteen thousand, wholesale."

"Why haven't you sold it then?"

"Because, as you are doubtless aware, these clocks are only suitable for a very rare buyer with a great deal of money and an elegant home with high ceilings. One never knows how long it will be before such a buyer turns up."

"But I am here. Now."

"Yes, but the most generous appraisal of these strings of pearls would be two or three thousand for the two lesser strings, and perhaps five thousand for the best one. You are asking me to accept a several thousand dollar loss."

"We discussed all this by email. I thought you were ready to deal."

"I was. I mean, I am, of course, but can't you please sweeten this with a little cash?"

"Of course not. A deal's a deal."

"But, Mr. Wingate, the whole point of me selling you this clock is that I need money, now, for medicine and to pay somebody to mind the shop while I go into the hospital again."

"You can sell the pearls if you need money."

"The only way I can get money immediately would be to sell them at far below market value, and that would hardly be enough for my treatment."

"We made a deal. What more do you want?"

"Please, can't you spare a couple of thousand extra, to even the score a little for me?"

"Why should I do that?"

"Because we're in the same business. We're colleagues. You never know when I might run across something that might interest you. And, besides, you are making an easy eight, maybe ten thousand here already."

"No."

"Okay. Then instead, would you please take a look around the shop for a few minutes. Perhaps there is something else you would like. I could give it to you on very favorable terms."

"I don't want anything else. I want the clock, and I consider the pearls to be more than fair payment. You have cancer. You need help. I'm helping you."

The old man's right hand began to tremble again and he placed it on the jewelry counter to steady it. He suddenly looked paler than he had earlier, and for a moment Wingate worried that he'd gone too far, that the geezer would crumple on the spot. "Okay," the shopkeeper said, his eyes beginning to fill with tears, "You win. I'll write up a slip for you."

Later, as Wingate sat in his car waiting for the ferry to load, he began to laugh. His laughing grew into a happy chorus with himself. His victory was that sweet.

Forty-fifth

The fax was grainy almost to the point of illegibility. Callahan should have expected as much from a newspaper picture, which in papers printed decades ago would have been grainy even when fresh off the press. Despite the limitations of the picture Felicia provided, the match with the morning's snapshot was pretty good, or at least that's what Callahan thought. Again he began to doubt his objectivity. Was he doing as he warned Willie not to do—falling in love with his pet theory? As he pondered his next move, there was a knock at the door.

"Hi, Mr. Callahan."

"You're out?"

Monty smiled. "Yeah, they finally realized that the story about me towing a body on an inner tube was too outlandish to be true. They found out from a neighbor that Carter Wingate has always hated me, so they decided he concocted the whole yarn as a prank to get me in trouble. Which, of course, is exactly what he did, and it worked."

"Felicia will be so relieved."

"I called her already. She's on her way up as soon as she can pack and lock up the house."

Callahan described his suspicions about Carter Wingate and showed Monty the pictures. He also suggested that Monty avoid going home right away. "If he discovers you've been released, he'll realize he may be next, and make run for it."

"He won't be next." Monty frowned. "That's why I stopped here first." He explained that he'd been given a private message for Callahan from Willie Custis, who drove him to the county lot to retrieve his car. A Virginia BCI agent recently assigned to the case said the sheriff's investigators were overlooking the obvious suspect—Callahan himself. After all, he claimed he found the body under his dock, but he could have killed Hazel Jones and then staged the whole discovery scene. As a former cop, he would have known how to make it look as if her body had drifted to his dock, when in fact he put it there. He lived only a couple of blocks from Duck's Restaurant and he owned a boat. His sudden closeness to Felicia suggested to the agent that he and Felicia knew each other *before* the murder, and that in fact it was a contract killing—perpetrated by Callahan so Felicia could inherit her mother's property.

"What's that man been smoking?"

"The agent's a woman, Willie says."

"How long have I got?"

"They could send someone any time."

"Shit!"

"Say, Mr. Callahan, how about if I stay at your house to wait for Felicia? As you said, it will keep Wingate from getting nervous, and if he's really Charlie Walton, I would rather she didn't get near him again."

"Good plan. Very good. Now, since you're staying, you can help me with a couple of things. First, tell me everything you know about Carter Wingate."

"That'll be easy. Almost nothing. He was living next door when I bought the lot to build my house, and he was very resentful about it. He had wanted to buy it himself and the owner, who happened to be a great aunt of mine, refused sell to him because, she told me, he gave her the creeps. When she died a little while later and they settled her estate, I was seeking a rural place to live, so I gave the legacy she left me to the other heirs in exchange for the land.

"Wingate travels fairly often, and sometimes brings home pieces of antique furniture or paintings. Occasionally guys in vans come and deliver such things. At least a couple of times I've seen people carry antiques out of his house. Also, a few times I've received his mail by mistake, and it's had magazines about antiques, coins, and collectibles."

"So maybe he's retired and collects antiques as a hobby, or maybe deals?"

"I guess it could be, but he's never confided that to me."

There was a knock at the door. "Mr. C? Are you home?"

"Hi, Willie, come on in."

"Official business, Mr. C. You'd better come out."

Callahan went to the door and saw through the screen a very anxious looking Willie Custis, Jr., and a tall, blonde woman in a gray suit. "Mr. Edward Callahan?"

"That's me."

"Special agent, Charlotte McCloskey, BCI." She flipped a badge so quickly Callahan saw nothing but her wrist movement. "We'd like you to come with us for a short interview."

"Am I being arrested?"

"Not if you cooperate."

He turned. "Monty, can you come here a sec?"

With Monty standing beside him, Callahan made agent McCloskey repeat that he would not be arrested and would be returned home that night after questioning. He knew he had already irritated her by obtaining another witness to her statement, but he didn't care. In fact, he decided to rub it in. He gave Monty a couple of twenties and asked him to walk up the street to Mario's for some pizzas and salads for dinner. "See you around six," he said, as if he, not the BCI or the sheriff's office, would determine when he would be home. Only then did he open the screen door.

* * *

Home again, and satisfied that he had put off the investigators for at least a few hours, but disappointed by their lack of interest in his Wingate equals Walton theory, Callahan found Monty sitting on his front porch reading one of Doris's many bird books.

"I had no idea you were so interested in birds," said Monty. "You have a terrific library."

"My late wife, Doris, was the birder."

"I wish I'd met her. These are seriously fabulous books."

"You would have liked Doris. She was incredibly knowledgeable about birds, but I paid no attention. She enjoyed talking to anyone who liked them."

"I got one vegetarian pizza, okay?"

"What's the other one?"

"Sausage and mushrooms, with green peppers and black olives."

"Perfect. Let's eat."

During dinner, Callahan asked Monty to try to remember anything else he could about Carter Wingate, but very little useful information resulted. Wingate almost never had visitors who weren't there for obvious commercial reasons, such as to mow the lawn or deliver packages. He kept to himself unless it was to complain about something Monty did, like playing his guitar late in the evening on his porch, which Wingate claimed upset the dog. Monty was out the night Hazel Jones died, so he couldn't say whether Wingate was home that night or not. Callahan concluded he would need to wing it. He would pay a call on Wingate the next day and try to talk his way in.

Monty turned in early, saying he was so glad to be sleeping outside the county jail that he wanted to start right away. Callahan realized that sleep would be the best preparation for what he'd planned for the next day, but he couldn't make himself feel sleepy. He sat and fidgeted in front of the TV, not even slightly attracted by anything showing. Disgusted with himself for wasting time, he headed for his wood shop. He knew very well that sanding and refinishing his coffin would be better done in daylight, but he needed some activity now.

He set up some lights at low angles to make it easier to see progress, and started a gentle sanding all over. As he went, he saw minor imperfections in the previous finish and tried to sand them out. It was not easy, and if he rubbed too vigorously, the finish became soft and gummed up the sandpaper rather than being scored lightly as intended. He decided that this coat of finish would be his worry coat. If it didn't turn out well, he would have to sand it off and repeat later.

After dusting carefully with his tack cloth, he applied a coat of finish as evenly as he could. The artificial light made it easy to see where he had been and the spots he missed. That was one advantage to nighttime working. A few minutes shy of midnight, he finished applying the finish. He cleaned his brush and sealed the can of finish tightly. As a side benefit of his labor, he finally felt tired and ready to sleep.

A Coffin for Callahan

As he turned to go, he noticed a moth, stuck in the finish and struggling to fly. Carefully he lifted it off the surface of the coffin lid with a putty knife, but now it was stuck to the knife blade. He thought of trying to pull it off, but realized it would probably fly back and land on the coffin lid again. He turned out all the lights and went outside. The moon had set hours ago and he could barely see. He gently lifted the moth by both wings and let it go.

Forty-sixth

The last chore on Wingate's to-do list proved to be the hardest. As soon as the detailing guys left, he could not escape: he had to deal with Orion. While it was certainly possible to take him along in a carry-on pet container, or to board him somewhere and have him shipped later, all the paperwork required to get him into Panama would increase the ways Wingate himself could be traced. Each time he moved to a different country, he would leave more documentation in his wake. He couldn't take the chance. Orion had to go, but where?

Wingate's feelings about his dog were conflicted. He cared for him—more than he liked to admit, because he didn't view himself as emotionally vulnerable—but he also resented the hold Orion had on him. One thought was a mercy killing: put him down (by what means he wasn't sure) and bury him next to the only house he had ever known. He dismissed the idea quickly, realizing that he didn't have the nerve to do it and if someone saw him, they might wonder about it. He'd been careful to give the appearance that he was only going on a two-week vacation; killing his dog would undo that effort.

Another idea was to put him in the boarding place where he usually stayed, but never pick him up. The owners were responsible locals who would not let Orion starve. They probably would find a good home for him somewhere. But they also might contact Animal Control or some other government agency first, thereby attracting attention to the fact that the dog's master had fled the country (in the unlikely event nobody had noticed already). Finally, he could drop Orion off at the SPCA, where he would be well cared for and eventually adopted by somebody. That seemed to be the lowest risk option.

After filling out the necessary paperwork and leaving his pet, he hurried to the car and went straight home, where he had a stiff drink—from a bottle of hundred dollar single malt scotch that he was also very sorry to be leaving behind. That evening, he made a simple dinner, packed a couple of bags with the best of his tropical wear, and went to bed early.

Forty-seventh

Callahan's rest was brief. Always a light sleeper, especially after passing the fifty-year mark, he awoke at about 3 a.m. to hear a car door slam, two women talking animatedly in his driveway, and a small dog barking. Before he could get to the window to see who was outside, there was a faint tapping on his front door. In a mental fog, he found his bathrobe and stumbled down the stairs, arriving in time to see Monty open the door wide to reveal Felicia, an overjoyed Thoreau, and Abigail Lee standing on his porch.

Thanks to Doris's careful arrangement of household things, he quickly found sheets, a blanket, and a pillow for Abigail and Thoreau to sleep together on the couch. Having been informed that Felicia and Monty "didn't mind sharing," he was urged not to worry, and that everything would be explained in the morning. Bidding goodnight to his house full of people, he trudged upstairs to bed, expecting to worry plenty, but surprising himself by sleeping well.

Awakened by the smell of coffee and noises from the kitchen, Callahan dressed as quickly as he could and went downstairs. Breakfast was ready, complete with some blueberries for his cereal that Felicia had brought.

The promised explanation of Abigail's presence was short, if not simple. A few days after Callahan and Felicia left the Green Pastures Endless Love Church, Abigail mentioned to her parents Felicia's offer to help her apply to an industrial design school. This news quite unexpectedly (to Abigail, but not Callahan) precipitated a huge family quarrel. Up to that point in her young life, Abigail, unlike many teenagers, had never had much trouble with her parents. The conflict was a revelation. The Reverends Lee became almost hysterical at the prospect that their daughter might go to New York and spend extended time with Felicia Jones. Abigail had never seen them snarl before. Shocked and hurt, she took what little money she had saved and a raincoat, walked down the long driveway out of her parents' church compound, her home for most of her young life, and thumbed a ride to the nearest small town. Then she called Felicia.

"What do your parents think of you running away?" asked Callahan.

"They don't know. Well, naturally they know, because I'm not home, but I haven't spoken to them since I left."

"You mustn't let them suffer like that. Call them, even if you never intend to go back."

"I will. Later."

"Let me tell you a little history, which I believe will help you understand your parents' feelings." Callahan explained how Charlie Walton had probably killed Abigail's grandmother and how, as Carter Wingate, he had more than likely killed Felicia's mother also. Next he showed her the pictures he had of the two men. He conceded that his belief that they were one in the same might be wishful thinking. Then he took a chance and said he thought Abigail's mother knew something about the first murder that she had been hiding for twenty-five years.

"That doesn't sound like Mom. She's always been very open about everything with us kids. You can ask her anything."

"Maybe, since you need to call her anyway, you could call her and ask her if my guess is right."

A Coffin for Callahan

She gave a pained look and raised her hand toward her mouth as if about to chew a fingernail, but quickly put both hands in her lap. "First, may I check something? Do you have a scanner?"

"A what?"

"A scanner for your computer, for copying pictures and things. You have a computer, right?" The look on her face suggested she might be talking to a cave man.

Callahan admitted that he had a computer, but had no idea of its capabilities beyond web searches and email, neither of which he used without Mrs. Davis's help. He showed Abigail where the computer was, and said if she knew how to use it she could do whatever she liked with it. She took the two original newspaper photos from Felicia and sat down to work. Monty suggested that he, Callahan, and Felicia could take Thoreau out for his morning walk.

They had barely reached the sidewalk when Mrs. Davis rushed across the street. She hugged Felicia and welcomed her back to Port St. George. She looked at Monty warily, until he explained that he'd been released, not escaped. Then she turned to Thoreau "What a cute little dog!"

"He's Thoreau," said Felicia."

"So charming, and friendly." She let Thoreau approach and lick her hand. "My friend Anne is so happy. She adopted a new dog today."

"The whole town worships the dog," said Monty.

"How true, and this town, especially. Do you like sayings, too? There's so much good wisdom in sayings."

"It's only a fragment of something I remember from a college class."

"The other part is 'but nobody worships chastity,'" she said confidently. Obviously pleased with herself, she continued, "Of course, that's actually not true, at least in Port St. George. Here many people take chastity very seriously. Naturally, there are some people . . . ." She looked at Felicia and blushed.

"What kind of dog did your friend buy?" asked Callahan, hoping to move the conversation along so they could continue walking and leave Mrs. Davis behind.

"A Scottie. But she didn't even buy it. She was so lucky. She has had a black Scottie for years and she'd always wanted a white one, and she'd told the people at the SPCA to be on the lookout. Yesterday they found exactly what she wanted and called her. Luck favors the well prepared."

"Pretty good break," said Monty.

"It was amazing. Apparently this man came in and dropped off a beautiful white Scottie. He'd had all his shots and everything. The man said he was sorry to see him go, but was unable to keep him."

"Did she say who the man was?" asked Callahan.

"What difference does that make, Edward? She got a lovely dog for free, just like she wanted. You can't beat free."

Callahan suggested they get on with the walk. He was in a hurry to return home where he could sit and think. Time seemed to be speeding up, and he was concerned that he would not be able to sort out his thoughts before events overtook him. After a quick tour that included showing Felicia the bakery, post office, and movie theater, Thoreau did what was expected of him, and they could return home.

A Coffin for Callahan

As soon as they arrived, Abigail approached Callahan. "May I show you something?" She laid a much enhanced version of the old newspaper photo of Charlie Walton down on the kitchen table. On top of the first print, she laid a black and white copy of the photo Callahan took the day before. "Hold them up to the light."

Callahan did as directed. "It looks like a single picture, a perfect match. How did you do that?"

"To be truthful, Mr. Callahan, you sounded kind of crazy to me when you said the same man may have killed both my grandmother and Mrs. Jones, so I scanned the newspaper photo—didn't know your printer also scans and makes copies did you?—and tried matching the light and dark tones, eliminating color, matching the chin to forehead distance, and softening the graininess in the old photo, and—voilà!"

"I believe it's time we called your mom."

"I know, but I don't want to." She went and sat on the porch, then got out her phone and stared at it as if it were radioactive.

After a few minutes, Abigail returned and handed her phone to Callahan. "She wants to talk to you now."

Callahan took the phone into his living room where he could be alone. The conversation was short and to the point. Reverend Lee confirmed what Callahan suspected. He went first to Felicia. "After speaking with Abigail's mother, I can tell you for certain that your father had nothing whatever to do with Mrs. Lambert's death—as your mother had always believed. I will explain it someday, but right now I have to go see Mr. Wingate."

Felicia wrinkled her eyebrows. "Shouldn't you call the police?"

"At the moment, I'm currently their prime suspect. If I tell them to go arrest Wingate, or that I'm going to visit him myself, they'll probably arrest me instead, and while they waste time questioning me, he'll escape. I can't take the chance."

The phone rang. Callahan reached for it and then looked at Monty. "You take it."

Monty picked up the phone and then covered the receiver. He looked anxiously at Callahan. "It's Deputy Willie Custis again. He says they want to interview you again and he's coming over to pick you up."

"I'm going to Wingate's house—now. Tell them I'm not here."

"Can't you wait and explain everything to Willie or the detectives?"

"There's no time. I believe the Scottie dog Mrs. Davis's friend got was Wingate's. He's getting ready to bolt—permanently—or he wouldn't have parted with his dog. He may be gone already." Callahan headed for the door.

"I just remembered, Deputy Custis, that Mr. Callahan is out walking my dog. I'm sure he'll be home in a little while." said Monty, and hung up.

Last

As he turned onto the five-mile stretch of road leading to Finley's Bar, Callahan conceded to himself that he didn't really know what he planned to do—question Wingate? Try to arrest him? Attack him? Normally, especially as he had gotten older, he liked to think things through before acting, but there was no time. He would have to confront the man and make it up as he went along. He thought briefly about what might happen in a physical confrontation, and comforted himself that Wingate appeared to be roughly his age, and probably wasn't as capable of holding his own in a fight. Then he realized that probably he wasn't in any better shape than Wingate and it might be close to an even match.

* * *

Wingate paced the floor. He had packed even more carefully than his customary punctilious way, and had dispersed his cash in his luggage and carry-on items and in a patent snakeskin money belt he bought many years ago. In his view the belt was tacky and not at all his style, but it was exquisitely designed to not look like the piggy bank it was. It had fooled more than one customs official in its time. Every door and window in the house was locked except the front door. The moving company would arrive next week and empty the place. All Wingate had to do now was sit tight until the limo driver arrived. Within less than three hours he would be in the plane, on his way—Miami, Panama, and who knows where after that—but he would be free, and safe for good. Even if the sheriff's office buffoons held Monty Bergman for only another twenty-four hours, that would be more than enough. They might eventually figure out that Wingate had killed Hazel Jones, and they might even discover where he'd gone, but so what? He was going to Central America, where moving from one small country to another is easy and money buys silence and obfuscation from politicians and police—and he had plenty to spend if he needed to.

The doorbell rang. The sense of relief that Wingate felt, believing that his ride had arrived, nearly took his breath away. Striding quickly, he went to the door and opened it. The man standing there did not look like a limo driver, and there was no limo in his driveway, but instead a shabby blue pickup truck that looked like it could use a good wash. "What do you want?" he asked.

The visitor glanced down at the two suitcases and carry-on bag sitting on the front steps. "Hello, Charlie. Planning a little trip?"

"You must have the wrong address. I'm not Charlie."

"Wrong. I've done my homework. You're Charlie Walton, killer of a bookkeeper named Mrs. Lambert in 1981 and of Hazel Jones two weeks ago."

"You're mad! Get off my property or I'm calling the police."

"Go ahead—call. I'm not going until you leave here in handcuffs, so you'll save me the trouble."

* * *

Callahan stood firm until Wingate tried to slam the door in his face. After seeing Wingate up close and watching the look in his eyes at the mention of the killings, Callahan lost all doubt about his identification. He stiff-armed the door back at Wingate, knocking him backward against a chair. "Go ahead, call."

"Whoever you are . . ."

"Callahan. Ed Callahan. I'm the one who found Hazel Jones's body."

". . . you're making a mistake. Yes, I once used the name Charlie Walton, but I had nothing to do with either killing. You're spouting nonsense, conjecture, theories . . . you're wasting both our times."

Callahan stepped into the house and closed the door behind him. "Wrong again, Mr. Wingate. Today I spoke with a highly credible witness who, after many years of silence, will provide Robert Jones with an alibi. He was not at the plant the night Mrs. Lambert died, yet someone who was there claimed to have seen him. That someone was you."

"Anyone else working there could have killed her and framed Bob."

"Factory people didn't go into the offices where Mrs. Lambert worked. You were the only senior staff member present, and you discovered the body."

* * *

Wingate knew he was cornered, but he'd been cornered before and found a way out, so all he had to do was buy time until his instinct for self-preservation kicked in and provided a solution. He might need to kill this Callahan guy, too, and all would work out fine if nobody came looking until he was safely on the plane. Or maybe he could talk his way out. He was confident he could do either, but needed time to develop a plan. "I don't believe we've ever met, Mr. Callahan, but I'm sure I've seen you somewhere before."

"My picture was in the paper after I found the body of Mrs. Jones."

"I've been out of town and haven't caught up on all the papers."

"And I came out here by boat yesterday and snapped a photo that proved very helpful in your identification."

"You had no right to snoop."

"You're a killer, Mr. Wingate, and my snooping proved it."

A plan was beginning to form. "Okay, I'll call the police if you like. But may we go into my study? The phone is there and my legs give me trouble if I stand in one place for a long time." Without waiting for an answer, Wingate went down the wide front hallway and turned left into a large room. Callahan followed closely behind and stood in the doorway. The room was dominated by a magnificent mahogany desk, surrounded by extensive bookshelves lining all the walls but one. Wingate went behind the desk and sat down with his back to the window. "Please, Mr. Callahan, take one of the leather armchairs. Relax."

"I prefer to stand," said Callahan. "Make your call."

"You have no authority. In fact, I believe you're making this all up as you go along. You came here on a whim to carry out some deranged fantasy of arresting me for two murders I did not commit."

* * *

Callahan watched as Wingate sat down calmly behind the desk. It was clear this guy had nerve, and he was trying to take control. As a former cop, Callahan knew he should not allow this to happen, but he was not sure how to stop it. He was rusty, and it showed. "Call," he said again.

"What if I don't? What if, when my limo comes, I simply hop in and let it whisk me away?"

Callahan pulled his long retired Glock 17 from his jacket pocket. He hadn't fired the weapon except in mandatory target practice since he shot the teenager in North Philadelphia in 1983. He'd only fired it once after moving to the Eastern Shore—to reassure himself it still worked. When he picked it up today before leaving the house, he couldn't remember whether the magazine had cartridges in it or not, and on the drive to Finley's Bar he'd forgotten to check. He didn't intend to use it today anyway, so whether it was loaded or not hardly mattered. "Call."

"What are you going to do, shoot me? You have no authority to do anything, and we both know it."

Unfortunately, what Wingate had said was true. As Wingate spoke, Callahan saw a patrol car pull into the driveway and Willie Custis, Jr. get out. After a quick, loud knock, the deputy opened the front door of the house, and shouted, "Mr. C, are you here?"

"In the back," Callahan shouted.

Willie appeared in the doorway of Wingate's study. He looked at Wingate, then at Callahan. "What's going on?" Callahan quickly explained his belief that Wingate and Walton were same person—and a double murderer. Willie looked puzzled, then distressed. "Mr. C, you'd better put your gun away. I'm here to take you in for Mrs. Jones's murder."

Wingate rose from his chair and smiled broadly. "Thank you, Deputy Custis, for rescuing me from this unfortunate situation. I have a plane to catch, so I'm going outside to wait for my limo. If I'm gone when you finish, do please lock the front door on your way out." He brushed past a helpless Callahan and a bewildered Willie Custis, Jr. and left the room.

"Hand me your gun, Mr. C. I won't cuff you if you agree to come along without a fuss."

Callahan turned over the Glock. "This is bullshit, Willie. A murderer is going to walk because of your department's idiocy."

"Come with me now, Mr. C., and you can explain it to them in Accomac."

* * *

Halfway to the front door, Wingate finally had the inspired thought he'd been waiting for. Overhearing that Callahan was suspected of murdering Hazel Jones set his mind working. If he acted quickly, he could execute his plan before his ride arrived. If he succeeded, he would ensure his safety forever. It would be so easy, and too delicious to pass up—two men, two guns—a work of art.

He ducked into the hall closet to await his opportunity. He could hear clearly as the deputy and Callahan talked in the study, and he contorted his body in his hiding place so would be able to see them approach. For the first time in his life, he prayed that a limo would be late. After a few moments, he heard them coming. As he had hoped, Callahan was first, followed by Deputy Custis holding Callahan's Glock, carefully aimed toward the floor.

As they passed the closet, Wingate slipped out silently, and in one smooth motion that a ballerina would envy, he snatched the deputy's gun from its holster. So focused was he on his plan that it did not cross his mind that there might be a retaining strap, but as it happened he accidentally did what the deputy was trained to do—push the strap forward with his thumb, releasing the pistol in an instant. Before Willie could react, Wingate grabbed his neck with his left hand and pointed the gun at the startled deputy's right ear. "Now I want Callahan's gun," he said.

* * *

Callahan turned and instantly assessed the situation. "No, Willie, toss my gun to me, here." He held out his hands, beckoning.

"Give it to me," Wingate demanded.

"To me, Willie—*now*, or he'll kill us both." He took a step forward. He was about eight feet away from Willie Custis, Jr., whose face had frozen into a mask of pure panic, his unblinking eyes hovering over a pleading, faintly ridiculous smile. As Callahan tried desperately to think of what to do next, Willie suddenly pitched the Glock forward in a gentle underhand toss. Surprising himself with his dexterity, Callahan caught the pistol and quickly achieved a firing grip. He raised the weapon and pointed it Wingate's face.

A Coffin for Callahan

"Drop the deputy's gun, Wingate. You're done."

* * *

Wingate's confidence was draining from him. He gazed into Callahan's eyes, one of which was at the opposite end of a gun sight pointed straight at his nose. His plan had failed, and he wasn't sure what to do next. But, as he'd done when cornered before, he would try a bluff. If it failed, he could always surrender and try something else later. "No. You give me your gun, Callahan, or this kid dies."

* * *

"You can't take out both of us," said Callahan. His mind raced. How have you managed to do this again? he asked himself. Once more, your poor judgment has put a fellow officer's life on the line. He looked into the eyes of Wingate and saw fear and contempt—a cornered predator who thought of nothing but his own well-being. Clearly, he was beyond reasoning with, and would stop at nothing to save himself. Praying that there were bullets in the magazine and that Willie would stand still, Callahan squeezed the trigger. Wingate's face disappeared from view as he fell backward, dropping Willie's gun to the floor. Callahan fired two more shots past Willie's rigid frame at the motionless body on the floor.

"Jesus . . ." whispered Willie, as he collapsed onto the floor like punctured brown balloon.

". . . Mary and Joseph," said Callahan, reaching in his pocket for his cell phone while the stream of blood from Wingate's shattered skull crept slowly toward his feet across a forty-thousand dollar oriental carpet.

END

About the Author

Haydon Rochester, Jr. was born in New York City and raised in the village of Hardwick in northern Vermont. After training as a natural scientist and employment as a scientific editor, he changed direction and began earning his living as a free-lance technical and marketing writer. In this capacity, he has written or edited approximately 120,000 pages of documents on topics ranging from mainframe computer systems to constipation.

Responding to a client's observation that his contribution to a government-sponsored report appeared to be largely fictional, Mr. Rochester began writing fiction as a hobby in 1985. Since then he has authored numerous short stories and six novels.

Since 2004 Mr. Rochester has lived in the charming town of Onancock, on Virginia's Eastern Shore.